THE REVELATION
OF NUMBER 10

THE REVELATION OF NUMBER 10

A Galactic Neighbor's Appeal

CLIFF JOSEPH

THE REVELATION OF NUMBER 10
A GALACTIC NEIGHBOR'S APPEAL

iUniverse books may be ordered through booksellers or by contacting:

iUniverse
1663 Liberty Drive
Bloomington, IN 47403
www.iuniverse.com
1-800-Authors (1-800-288-4677)

Because of the dynamic nature of the Internet, any web addresses or links contained in this book may have changed since publication and may no longer be valid. The views expressed in this work are solely those of the author and do not necessarily reflect the views of the publisher, and the publisher hereby disclaims any responsibility for them.

Any people depicted in stock imagery provided by Getty Images are models, and such images are being used for illustrative purposes only.
Certain stock imagery © Getty Images.

ISBN: 978-1-5320-4225-6 (sc)
ISBN: 978-1-5320-4226-3 (e)

Library of Congress Control Number: 2018901578

Print information available on the last page.

iUniverse rev. date: 03/13/2018

Cover designed by Zuri Joseph

Chapter 1

✳ ⎯⎯⎯ ✳ 🌐 ✳ ⎯⎯⎯ ✳

THE IMPOSTOR
IN THE SKY

Hi! I'm Mark DeLouise, and I've got quite a story to tell. It's going to take a little time. So maybe you would like to find a nice quiet place to relax before I get started.

Are you ready? Okay! It began in the wee hours of a hot and sultry Saturday morning. It was late August, 1998, and two am in New York City. The sounds of week-end Westbeth parties competed with my insomnia, vying for which could most effectively keep me from much needed sleep. Beside me, the sounds of Gracie's deep-sleep breathing seemed to accompany the cacophonous mix of jazz, rock, and reggae. Nagging concerns over issues of work and relationships, guilt from mundane failures brought feelings of insult and self punishment. Restless summer nights, restless any season nights. Nothing new. At other times, I had simply accepted it, got up and read or painted or tried to write a poem. If this didn't work, I might turn on the TV, keeping the sound low so I wouldn't disturb Gracie.

This night, however, was different. Oddly different. I got up, but it never entered my mind to follow my usual distractions. Instead, as if hypnotized, I was drawn toward our windows, surveying northwest a view of New Jersey and northeast, midtown Manhattan, with the

Empire State Building about a mile away. The sky was indigo-blue-black; clear with as many stars as an urban sky can allow. Over the Jersey side, one in particular drew my attention. I looked in wonderment because I had never seen such a star. Although a star-ignorant New Yorker, I questioned whether or not this really was a star. It was bigger and brighter than any I had ever seen even when I traveled west. As deprived as I was of night-sky knowledge, however, I was familiar with certain formations, and I knew how to spot Venus and Mars. This light was not a plane or hovering helicopter or even a weather satellite. I watched for several minutes. It did not move.

The sounds that had competed to keep me awake seemed to subside, in part because of my intense shift from irritation to wonder, but also in fact. I had stood at my window star-gazing for nearly an hour. It was now about 3 am. The rock sounds had ceased, while the reggae had become mellifluous, merging with cool jazz. I conjured up an image of what the few remaining in the party crowds might be doing. My thoughts shifted to Gracie, still fast asleep. I had been annoyed that she could sleep so well while I tossed and turned, but then I was struck with the passion I felt for her.

As my gaze stayed riveted on the mysterious star; without a spoken word, I wished that she was awake to gaze at it with me. What happened next more than confirmed my belief in mental telepathy, because seconds later, I heard her voice,

"Man, what are you doing? Why did you call me?" Half asleep, she stumbled toward me.

For a moment I was speechless. Recovering my senses, I replied. "You're awake! ... No, no, I didn't call. ... But you must come here. You must look!"

She came and stood by my side, grabbing my arm with one hand, and rubbing her sleepy eyes with the other. The issues of our working lives that too often obscured the magic of our love seemed to disappear. In our space lit only by outdoor lights, I brought the image of her full beauty to mind. She was slender; about five feet, four, with classic curves, reminding me of the Greek Aphrodite. The peach glow of her face, hazel eyes, long brown hair and Anglo facial feature could not mask her cheek bones hinting of native American genes. Her beauty and mine. Our differences made us both feel beautiful. I was about five feet, eight, and also slender. Dark sub-Saharan skin, West African facial feature and woolly hair was my contrasting image. Gracie had encourage me to grow a beard, which made us both happy.

"I heard you call," she said. "I heard you call loud! ... And I was fast asleep."

As I gazed skyward, she came to the window. "What are you looking at? What do you want me to see?" At this hour, her tone suggested, it better be good.

Pointing, I asked Gracie if she had ever seen a star like that. She knew immediately which one I meant.

"Never. Not even in the desert."

Seemingly responding to her recognition, the "star" zipped across the sky southeast toward us. In less than a minute, it was right over our neighborhood. We looked at each other in amazement.

"Hey," I said. "That had to be ..."

"A UFO!" In awe, Gracie finished my thought.

The star had held its position until my partner could share witness. And now that it was so close, we could see that it was round and circled with flashing blue and white lights. We stood a moment in silence.

"This is not something we can talk about. We need to wait." There was nothing more to say then, not even to ourselves. It was almost four am, so we went back to bed. Surprisingly, the strange phenomenon in no way interfered with our return to much needed sleep.

The next day, we stayed alert for confirmation of our sighting. Sharing our experience without public confirmation, even with our own daughter, seemed problematic. Sarah probably was open to such phenomena, but it would be only with careful thought that we would add this to her increasingly complex world. For years, she had been small for her age, but at nine, she was beginning to catch up with her average peer. Before we had moved to Westbeth, she had few playmates, but Westbeth now provided her with a multitude of friends, the offspring of families who shared our culture of creativity. No longer was her Afro out of place, no longer were her second hand clothes second rate.

She had been awake before us, working on a construction paper model of our solar system. As she worked, her pretty light brown face reflected seriousness. Her features were suggestive of mine at that age, although she was very feminine, and had her mother's eyes. How oddly timed, I thought, that the solar system would be her current school project. While making sure that all the planets were in proper relationship, she also was not ignoring the aesthetic aspects of her work. It was more than just science. Yes, she was probably ready to hear our story.

After brunch, Sarah went upstairs to pack the things she would need for a week-end visit to her friend Rachel's family country place. She was becoming quite independent, and looked forward to spending time with her friends. Adults must have seemed very boring. I thought about some of our dinner time conversations, when Gracie and I would discuss the problems of the world. Sensing how shut out Sarah may have felt, Gracie would sometimes shift our focus to Sarah's interests. Sarah could not have understood our complex references, but she had to have learned that much was wrong.

Soon Sarah was ready to leave. Gracie made sure that Sarah had everything she would need, and then went with her to meet Rachel and her family. Gracie would be back shortly, but I gave my big nine-year-old a hug, and wishes for a fun trip.

After they left, I turned my mind to work, even as our UFO experience had changed me forever. I still needed to get started on the last painting of my set of ten, for the *Ten of Each* exhibit, at Westbeth Gallery in less than a month. Usually, I am eager to start a new painting. Each one is a new adventure, a problem-solving challenge, an opportunity to creatively say what I need to say. My feeling now was unusually intense. It was as if I was being pushed and pulled into my studio, rather than moving on my own. Each of the nine completed paintings of my series focused on an aspect of oppression or injustice in our world. This tenth and last one was to be about homelessness. I had prepared for the painting with several sketches, which I tacked up on my studio wall as reference.

As I began to work on the linear structure of the composition, I felt that something strange was beginning to happen. I tensed up, and stood for a moment staring at the canvas. I was shocked and confused – what I had intended to draw was not what I was drawing. It was disturbingly evident that I was not in control of what was taking place. I stopped and tried to regain my composure. Then I tried again to lay the structure for my painting, but instead I was executing a work I knew nothing about. I felt a reminiscence of the wonder of the UFO night, but this time also fear. I felt shaken by my lack of control, but then my curiosity began to overcome fear. I began to relax. Now I was ready to explore; to co-operate instead of resist.

I was producing a mystery. I felt that the drawing was being done on my own power, but with a speed and in a manner that was not my own. I could hardly wait to see what image would develop. What emerged was totally unfamiliar, although it had flowed onto the canvas from my hand as though it were my own design. In no way could it ever have been my work. I might have identified it as the work of an architectural engineer equipped with drafting tools, not with only charcoal, brushes and paint. And even for such a professional, it would have taken days to finish. I stood back from the canvas; spell-bound, awe-struck, puzzled, ecstatic and still a bit scared. It was difficult to describe exactly what I was feeling. It was all of the above and more.

The structure on my canvas was a building with a cut-away section revealing a complicated, highly technical interior. I wondered if such a place existed. It certainly hadn't grown out of my imagination. Clearly, I was only the agent being used. But why? The structure had to be connected with the UFO visit. There was no other explanation. But was this some technological fortress from another planet, or did it depict something right here on Earth? I remembered the character in the movie, <u>Close Encounters</u>, who was compelled to build a scale model of the actual place where the space ship would land. Was this a proleptic vision, or was it some other ominous reference?

I heard Gracie's key in the door. My heart pounded, signaling my eagerness to share my experience with her. I could hardly wait for her to come down the stairs to show her what had happened, and ran up the stairs to meet her halfway. She had stopped for groceries on her way home and could use some help with the bags.

"You can't put things away just yet. Come into the studio!"

She must have sensed my urgency. Apparently, however, she had a need to resist. Whatever curiosity she must have had, she perhaps needed a moment to prepare for something that most likely would be weird.

"Let me just get the perishables in the 'fridge. I'll be there."

When she did come, she stared at the canvas with a look of incredulity.

"Mark! What is this?"

"A painting."

"Well, yes. But a painting of what? Where did it come from?"

"I did it."

"When?"

"While you were out."

"No, no. That's impossible. This is very detailed work. When I came in here this morning the canvas was blank. Now it's almost finished."

"It's the same canvas."

"Oh, come on. You don't work this way. You don't work this fast. And why would you do something like this? It isn't you. It doesn't relate to anything you've ever done. Who did it, Mark? Why is it here?"

As I explained the whole experience, Gracie had to have seen how overwhelmed I was. She took my hand. With awe, we stood together, questioning the work, wondering what might come next.

Then she broke away from me. "But you can't put this in the show. It doesn't belong. You still have to do another painting."

Another painting. I would try again to do the painting on the homeless. My semi-abstract style could capture the contradiction of want in this world of plenty. The painting would be less representational than my usual, to pull out deeper levels of understanding on the issue. I had believed that I could do an effective piece.

While Gracie returned to the kitchen, I attempted to remove the painting from my easel. It would not budge. I tried and tried, but I could not move this normally quite manageable four by six feet lightweight canvas. I called Gracie, who looked very puzzled when I asked for help. I attempted again to remove the canvas, so that Gracie could witness my dilemma. Knowing how easy it should have been, she tried removing it herself, and then we both tried together. Obviously, something very strange was going on. She gave my hand a gentle squeeze, which I read as her understanding. This had to be connected to our UFO sighting. Perhaps sensing that I might want to be alone, Gracie went back to her mundane tasks.

I stood quietly for a moment, wondering what to do. Soon I began to feel the same compelling push and pull that got me started on this mysterious painting. The urge was to continue. In spite of my intention to complete my series with a compatible expression, I could not resist this "force." Soon I was again involved with all my being in a work that was not my own. Less than an hour later, I called Gracie to come and see the finished work.

Gracie had resisted interrupting me earlier. She had been very curious. Considering what she had already seen, the painting could not have been a surprise. Still, she looked stunned all over again. "My God," she said. "Oh, my God. What is this power?"

"I call it the 'force,'" I replied. "And now I feel really drained. It is not my idea, but it has been my energy."

I had to rest. I knew that Gracie wanted to talk, but I was feeling numb. Assuring Gracie that I would be all right, I climbed into our loft bed. I must have gone to sleep as soon as my head hit the pillow.

About two hours later, I awoke; startled to see a marble-sized orb of light, hovering in space near the ceiling. I felt calmed. From my loft location, it was close enough to touch, but before I could sit up, it disappeared. Now the drained feeling that had sent me to bed was completely reversed. I felt a strange power, the source of which I credited to the strange orb of light.

What I had named the "force," had made possible a creation that I could never have imagined, but a profound depth of my own energy was also required. It had been a co-creative project.

The next day, Sunday, we woke up early, sharing our undefined mission. We had always tried to be conscientious people. Beyond relating to intimate responsibilities and the conventional demands of work and community, we tried to discern our reason for being. As an artist, I felt called to raise consciousness relating to the struggles of our time. Out of necessity, Gracie focused on more immediate concerns, but her patience made my work possible. There was a constant tension between the practical and the need to counter the culture we wished to change. Now we were being called for something we had yet to understand.

These tensions provoked the age-old need for Sabbath, a need that too often was either ignored or rendered inauthentic by the institutions that perpetuated it. But now we shared a truly Sabbath feeling.

As planned, we picked up the New York Times. We often did not bother getting the paper, especially not before eight o-clock, but now we anxiously bought the "paper of record," to see if the sighting had been "fit to print." We distrusted the mass media, but the Times was still our best bet for current local news.

We were not disappointed. UFO sightings were reported in the northeast Jersey area, in sync with the time of our experience. Now it would be easier to share our story with Sarah, even before we might think of anyone else who should know.

But what did this all mean? First, I had been mysteriously drawn to the window. Then Gracie, who had been really sound asleep, heard me call her, although I did not call. The "force" seemed to have picked us out, and waited for us to witness it together. It had even carried my thoughts to Gracie, using my voice. And now I had become an agent of their communication.

"We have been given a great responsibility."

"You were chosen," Gracie responded. "But chosen for what?"

"Chosen." That sounded very grandiose. Gracie's question was, of course, my question, too. But instead of feeling grandiose, I felt humbled. I thought about what I would tell Sarah when she returned home.

Sarah returned in time for supper. She arrived with Rachel and Rachel's mom, Alice. I was thankful that Sarah had friends who could give her the chance to get away. Sarah appreciated city life, but I felt that she needed to know that there was another world out there. Gracie and I thanked Alice and suggested that maybe we could take the girls to the planetarium soon. We said our good-byes, and Sarah settled back into her familiar surroundings. After supper, I suggested she come and see my new painting.

"What's that?!" she said as she walked into my studio. "It's not your painting!"

"It doesn't look like my work, does it?" But it is. I don't really know how I came to paint it. But your mother and I think that it relates to something that happened early Saturday morning while you were fast asleep."

I said that it had been a night when I had trouble sleeping. I told her how I had gotten up and looked out the window, and that her mother had joined me, and what we saw.

Excitedly she asked, "Was it a flying saucer, Dad? Was it?"

"You might call it that. We called it a UFO – an unidentified flying object. There was a strange looking light in the sky. I watched it hover over New Jersey. Then when your mother joined me, it sped right into our neighborhood. It seemed to be there especially for us, but other people saw it, too. Take a look at what the paper reported."

For Sarah, like most kids her age, there needed to be a really good reason to read the paper. This was a good reason. I showed her the article in the Times, which she read eagerly.

"Wow, I wish I had been there."

"It all happened so fast. We didn't really know what we were seeing until it was too late to wake you."

Sarah looked again at the painting. "And that's why you did this?

How does this connect with a UFO? And how did you do it so fast? This doesn't even look like what you do."

"I know. I guess our UFO experience inspired me in a strange way. But it is my painting."

I could not deny the UFO connection. Sarah could never accept the idea that it was just something I happened to paint. But she didn't need to know how overwhelming my experience was, either. She was not ready to press me at this point, but I could tell by the way she looked at me, and again at the painting before she walked away, that she had more questions.

Sarah offered to help her mother with the dishes. That was usually my job when Gracie was working, but as a school teacher, she had the summer off. Besides, I still needed to complete my series.

But regardless of my intentions, I again went to the window to look out where the mysterious star had appeared. Had it been my wish, as some telepathic communication, that had awakened Gracie out of a very sound sleep? I did have some belief in telepathy, but could telepathy have created my loud voice? Or had it been another force, perhaps the same "force" that directed me to create this alien painting?

Dusk had not yet yielded to darkness. A sliver of sundown amber stretched its glow across the western sky. The ether stage had not been set for heaven's performing stars. At first, our UFO had posed as just another star. I wondered if this impostor would return to steal the show again. I thought about others who might have witnessed this UFO, and wondered who else might have been contacted in such a special way. And why were we, and possibly others, selected? Why my architecturally drafted painting? Were other artists compelled to do similar work?

I recalled Ezekiel's vision of the chariot: "The spirit of the living creatures was in the wheels." Ezekiel's dream, a myth – symbols from the prophet's world, the glory of God and warning to His people. Ezekiel's wheels rose from the Earth, hovering beneath a dome of Divinity. "I saw something that looked like fire, and there was a splendor all around." Could his vision have been inspired by an actual sighting?

I thought about contemporary reports of strange things in our sky. In concrete language, aimed at more scientific minds, there were reports of landings and abductions. Some claimed that the U.S. Air Force had covered up evidence of sightings. Reports of this sighting were public, but my experience with it (and Gracie's) had so far been shared with no one but Sarah. We still had no idea what all of this would mean.

My determination to start the last painting of my series for the show waned. I spent the rest of the evening putting my studio in order.

On Monday morning I made one more attempt to complete my series. But again, when I tried to remove the mystery painting from my easel, it would not budge. I found myself walking, trance-like, to my drawing table. I picked up a dark blue marker there, walked behind the easel, and wrote, "Number 10" on the back of the canvas.

The message was clear. Whatever my intentions had been, they were now irrelevant. The "force" needed this painting to be in the show. However interesting this tenth painting was, it was unrelated to my series. I had no idea how I could explain it, and feared that it might cause me embarrassment. Angrily, I paced my studio. The painting was an imposition on my personal creativity. I felt confused and manipulated, subject to an alien force. I recalled my experience years before, working as a commercial artist, manipulated by the interests of corporate capitalism. I understood that manipulation, but this was an overwhelming puzzle. Now I was both hopeful and afraid.

Years back, responding to my growing socio-political consciousness, I walked away from Madison Avenue. I began to express my passion for justice on canvas, to be displayed in public spaces. My work was a protest against the Powers and Principalities, including the forces I used to serve.

I expressed my anger on canvas. My art spoke out against injustice, oppression and violence, and the complicity of bystanders. I wanted others to see what I saw. I promoted counterculture.

My art made some feel uncomfortable. So, in spite of laudatory notice from respected critics and demands to show at counter cultural exhibits, no one who could afford my work was likely to buy it. I wanted to change hearts and minds, but praise came mostly from the already converted. Even when my work was published, I felt frustrated because I could never reach enough people. Now I could not even control my own work.

The telephone jarred me out of my introspection. I answered, and a gentle but strong voice said, "Thank you." We were disconnected before I could ask any questions.

More mystery. More anxiety. Yet, I felt a potential for new power.

I looked at the clock. It was time to re-orient myself towards earning a living. Fortunately, I had developed a stable and salaried career in hospital work. I worked in New Jersey as a therapist, helping psychiatric patients to see in their own art work, the issues they needed to work on. At this point, I might have been questioning my own sanity, if Gracie had not been with me to witness my incredible experiences.

I was scheduled to be at the hospital at one o'clock. As I drove to work, I was still wondering about the mysterious phone call. Could it have been the "force," thanking me for my execution of the painting? As I reached the Jersey side of the Holland Tunnel, I tried to shove my question aside. Soon I would be asked to present my professional understandings at our weekly case conference. I prayed that I would not lose focus.

Sometimes, patients who participated in group mural sessions drew things which they described as "UFO's" or "flying saucers." These flight objects, and others, such as airplanes, space shuttles and rockets, might express a need to escape threatening situations experienced or imagined. At other times, objects from outer space might represent a magical, unrealistic solution to problems. In either case, my job was to help patients understand what was real and what their symbols meant, and find resources to move toward health.

Thinking about this, I was reminded that sharing my week-end experience with staff, would raise serious questions about my own sanity.

It was particularly difficult, however, to avoid my personal UFO thoughts, because the case I was going to present was a patient who had lead off a mural session by suggesting the theme, "Space Objects." The group had agreed, and had busily created comets, space ships and flying saucers.

At the conclusion of my presentation, the chief of service, Dr. Jonas, asked me how I responded to patients who claimed they had seen flying saucers. The total silence and the eyes riveted in my direction, told me that he had asked that question for everyone's benefit. I had to come up with a good, objective clinical response. Somehow, I was able to put my thoughts together quickly enough to cover my feelings of panic. When I found the courage to speak, I said, "Up to a week ago, in spite of the many books, articles and news reports documenting claims of sightings and abductions, as well as movies with which I'm sure you are familiar; I treated such claims with clinical skepticism. In matters of this kind, when dealing with psycho pathologically diverse cases, it is sometimes difficult to discern which side of the thin line between credible observation and visual hallucination a patient is on. If you saw Sunday's New York Times, however, you may have read of the UFO sightings just north of here. Such reports suggest that we reserve clinical judgment until a patient's claim regarding such phenomenon is weighed against other observations of his or her mental condition."

I had handled that challenge well. The expressions and nodding of heads in the group confirmed my competence. But I was not completely relieved until, when a couple of hands were raised, Dr. Jonas stood up and said," Folks, we've run overtime, so there will be no more questions. Let's thank Mark DeLouise for a most enlightening presentation."

As they applauded, I smiled, nodded my appreciation, and moved quickly toward the door; getting a few handshakes, pats-on-the-back, smiles and favorable comments. I had to move fast to avoid the two interns who had raised their hands to ask more questions. I needed to get to the restroom. Standing at the urinal, the concerns I brought to my case presentation were replaced by my worries relating to the upcoming Westbeth show.

Chapter 2

THE SIGHTING OF
NUMBER 10

A month later we were getting ready for the show's opening celebration. Gracie had gotten dressed ahead of time, but was now suggesting that she might change into something else. It was not like her to be so nervous in such a familiar context. And when little Sarah asked, "Are you alright, Dad?", I knew I had failed to hide my own anxiety. I anticipated a barrage of questions relating to my *Number 10*. How could I answer them?

Usually I was well prepared to respond candidly to questions about my art. Because I hoped that the work spoke for itself, I would point out elements in the work that would help viewers come to their own understanding. For some, the insights would come easily, but for others, existential limitations made it impossible for them to really "get it." But *Number 10* posed another problem. How could I explain what I did not understand myself?

When the three of us entered the gallery, we were greeted by two of our neighbors, Gail and Patrick. As we adults exchanged hugs, I wondered if my tenseness came through to them. If it did, I could not read their response. Their primary motive was to tell me what they thought of my work. Gail commented first,

"Mark, your work is as great as ever."

"I think it's better than ever, Mark," said Patrick. "Your social statements are both beautiful and jarring. *Number 10* is intriguing, but I have to admit a bit of a puzzle. Gail and I were trying to figure it out, but you'll have to help us."

I had known this was coming. Why had I not yet thought of a way to deal with it? "I'll have to get back with you on that one," I said, and left them talking to Gracie.

Sarah chose to follow me, until she caught sight of Rachel, and together they found the refreshment table. Continuing on alone, I positioned myself where I could observe, without being too obvious, the body language of viewers when they came to *Number 10*. I waited to see their double-takes and questioning stances. But when the gallery started filling up, observation became difficult. I decided to move in closer and eavesdrop on viewers' comments. That strategy didn't work, however, because as soon as I made my move, people who recognized me came swarming in with compliments and questions. The questions, of course, were difficult. For one who could usually concoct a plausible response when an authentic one seemed problematic, I became embarrassingly tongue-tied, until one of the viewers unwittingly gave me the answer I so desperately needed. She approached me saying,

"Excuse me, Mr. DeLouise. Someone pointed you out as the artist who painted this series. I just had to thank you for such powerful work. It is one thing to read about the world's profound injustice, but you really make me feel it. I will be noting that in the guest book, but that's not why I searched you out. I have to ask you about *Number 10*. How does it relate to your other work? Or am I correct in assuming that it's a mini preview; a heralding of your next series?"

Although I was hoping and praying I would never again have to go through the unwelcome experience of co-producing another painting like it, I said,

"Well, yes. You seem to be the first person to have figured that out – or at least the first person to tell me."

Thank God. I now had a much needed fabrication to respond

to my viewers, which I hoped would soon be spread as rumor. The absurdity of the "new series" made me feel uneasy, but it was much more manageable than the truth, which no one would believe. Later, of course, I could say that I changed my mind. My spirit felt a little lifted. I started to look for Gracie, but was interrupted by Gail.

"Oh, there you are, Mark! I finally found you."

"Hello. What's up?"

"There's a man here who is very interested in *Number 10*. He acts like he wants to buy it."

"It's not for sale."

"I know. But I think you should tell him that. He wants to meet you, so I said I would look for you, and left him there admiring the painting."

As we made our way through the hors d'oeuvres-snacking, wine-sipping crowd, Gail informed me that the man had come with Bill Osborne, our local congressman, who was a friend of Westbeth manager, Fran Lynd.

"There he is! See how he's examining the work. He must have lots of money."

Gail tapped him on the shoulder. "Sir, I didn't get your name, but this is Mark DeLouise, the artist."

The man turned toward us. "Oh, yes. Hello, there. My name's Burns. Dan Burns. I've been admiring your work, especially this one."

"Nice to meet you, Mr. Burns. Thank you."

I turned to introduce Gail, but she had suddenly disappeared into the crowd.

"Your friend seems to have found some old acquaintances," Burns said. "She left before I could thank her for tracking you down."

"We'll see her again. Meanwhile, Mr. Burns, why don't you and I get some wine? I expect she might happen by again any time."

Where was this man coming from? He did not seem like someone who would be interested in my work. I did not believe that he could relate to social protest, and I felt uneasy about his interest in *Number 10*.

"Wine would be good, thank you. And you can drop the 'Mr. Burns'. Call me Dan."

Our friendly facades were mutual covering for what I believed to be mutual suspicion. Dan continued, "I picked up a price list, Mark, and saw that *Number* 10 is not for sale. Why not?"

"That painting is the first of my next series, Dan. This may seem like an odd approach, but I decided to show it now, just to get people's reactions."

"Well, you sure got my attention. And the work seems to be getting a lot of other attention as well. Does this mean that I won't be able to buy it until after you have exhibited your whole series?"

"Essentially, yes, *if* I decide to sell it. And even then, you would have to contractually agree to loan me the painting whenever I exhibited the whole series." I was hoping that this would discourage him. After all, it was not really my painting.

Dan continued as if the deal had already been made. "Mark, if you don't mind, I'd like to take a picture of you standing next to *Number 10*. I'd like to show my wife what might be our future art acquisition, and the artist who painted it."

Although we had not even discussed price, I wasn't going to deny his request. He took six pictures before we resumed our path to the refreshment table. On our way, we met Gracie, Sarah and Rachel. When I introduced them, Dan's already ruddy complexion grew redder. I assumed that, in spite of the multicultural nature of our gallery scene, he did not expect me to have a white wife and that he was upset by such relationships. Gracie must have shared my thoughts on him, because she could barely mange a polite acknowledgment. She seemed relieved when Gail and her friends, and Patrick approached. Dan now called out to Gail and thanked her for our earlier introduction. More introductions were made, and then Sarah and Rachel quickly manged to escape the scene. Gail seemingly wasn't picking up anything off about Dan.

Congressman Bill Osborne and Fran Lynd spotted Dan, and joined our group, which had made *Number 10* its main topic. All the attendant questions were being directed at me. More friends and visitors kept coming over to make comments and ask questions. Fran and Bill had some other issue of concern, but could not get Dan's attention. As I was wondering how I could get away from all this, Gracie came to my rescue.

"Mark, don't forget that call you're expecting at ten. It's twenty of. Let's pick up Sara now so we can be there when the call comes in."

We said hurried good-byes, as Dan Burns called out,

"Mark, I'll be in touch."

Dan Burns looked forty-something, with reddish balding hair, dark brown eyes, and a broad- shouldered, six foot build that might have served him well on a football team. There was a trace of Scottish in the articulation of his words, especially when he talked excitedly. On the way home, I thought about how closely he was examining almost every detail of the strange building in *Number 10*, particularly its interior, with the machinery and complicated equipment. The painting was most everyone's focus in the show, but Burns' fascination for it went far beyond anyone else's. Yet, with all his great interest, he never asked the kinds of questions others were asking, like, "What building is that?" "Is it anywhere around here?" "What are all those gadgets?" Instead, he wanted to know if it was done from a photograph, and when I told him it wasn't, he asked searchingly,

"Well, where did you get the idea from? It's so detailed; it must have taken ages to do. It sure doesn't look like something you just dreamed up."

It was, of course, nothing that I had dreamed up, so at first I was relieved when he went on without waiting for my response. His next question, however, was not any easier.

"Mark, you're a message painter; social commentary and stuff like that. What's the message behind your *Number 10*?"

The Painting

10

I don't know why no one else had asked me that. I wanted to think of an answer, not just for Dan, but for anyone else who would wonder about it. I didn't know what to say, but to mask my embarrassment I said,

"My new series is an experiment. We artists sometimes like to express mystery. I am not yet sure how the other paintings will express it, but the universe is a mystery."

Of course I had no intention of doing more paintings like *Number 10* and prayed that no such work would be forced upon me. I did not say that the painting was a mystery to me as well.

Meanwhile I had to ask myself, why would Dan think that the painting had been done from a photograph? The thought that he might have some point of reference was more than I was prepared to think about. I pushed the question from my mind.

As we got off the elevator, Sarah asked for the keys so she could run ahead and get to the bathroom. Gracie and I took this opportunity to lag behind and share our thoughts.

"Very strange guy," said Gracie, not needing to explain who she meant.

"Very," I replied. "And I don't think its just paranoia. We know how *Number 10* got in this show. Burns seemed like a scary guy to begin with, but his interest in the painting makes him seem even scarier."

We pushed our fears aside as we entered our apartment. We spent a few minutes with Sarah, kissed her good-night and went to bed. On Saturday, refreshed from a late morning rest, I began a painting for a series on homelessness in an affluent society. I was interrupted by the phone. The Scottish sound in the "Hello, Mark" told me that Dan Burns was on the line.

Chapter 3

THE SETUP BEGINS

"Hi, Dan. What's up?"

"Mark, I have two reasons for calling. Jenny, my wife, would like to see the show – your *Number 10* in particular. I have my own darkroom, so I developed the picture I took of the painting and you. I did it this morning and it came out great. Jenny wants to see the real painting, since I told her I would like to buy it. She also wants to meet you. Ha-ha-ha, thinks you're quite a handsome guy. And we'd like to bring a couple of friends along. Tell me when it will be convenient for you to be there, so Jenny and our friends, the Carringtons, can meet you. It would be a special treat for them to meet the artist y' know."

I could not believe that Dan knew much about art. So what was his interest in *Number 10*? Why was he trying to get close on a personal level? He made me feel uncomfortable. But because I wanted to know where he was coming from, I would not turn him down.

"How about next Saturday, Dan? The gallery opens at ten and closes at six."

"Saturday would be fine. As a matter of fact, the Carringtons have already said Saturday would be best for them, and we'll come whatever time you say."

"Come at four. That will give you a couple of hours to see the

show. It's the best time for me because I like to paint early in the day when I get the best natural light. Weekends are when I do most of my painting."

"And why is that?"

"I work for a living, Dan. Five days a week."

"But of course! Forgive me for sounding like one of those folks who think artists have nothing to do all week but have fun making art. It's true for some, but I should have known that you didn't fit that category. We'll be there at four.

"And we'd also like to get together with you on Sunday in two weeks. Jenny and I have plans with the Carringtons then to see the Jacob Lawrence show at the Studio Museum in Harlem and then have supper afterwards at Billy's. We wanted to make it a family outing. As an African-American artist, you can explain Lawrence's work for us, and I'm interested in what you think of Billy's soul food."

"That's a possibility. I've been intending to see Jake's show, but the museum employs docents who can tell you a lot more about him and his work than I can. As for Billy's, the food is heavy on salt and fat, but there's probably something I could order. I'll let you know if we can make it when I see you Saturday."

Nothing about Dan seemed real. Why was he so motivated to connect with us? I could not imagine that his cultural interests went much beyond the arena of high profile sports, a few friends to share hamburgers and beer, and the satisfaction of winning a bet on his favorite team.

As for selling him my painting, I did not want it in his hands. As much as I needed the money, I would not sell him anything. But I needed to know what his interest in *Number 10* was. I was feeling more and more anxious.

Gracie shared my discomfort, but we avoided talking about it. She agreed, however, that we should join him and his family and friends on their Harlem jaunt. Seeing him interact with his family and friends might give us clues to our puzzle.

"I wonder what Mrs. Burns is like, Gracie said. "And what does a family outing mean? Do they have children?"

I shrugged. "Presumably. I'll find out Saturday."

"Please do. If there's no kid near her age, Sarah may not want to go."

"We'll see. Sometimes Sarah just likes to look at art. She won't like Dan either, but we don't know anything about his family and friends."

"I am beginning to get curious. I wish I could hang out with you Saturday and meet Mrs. Burns and the Carringtons, but I can't. That's the date when I'm finally taking Sarah and Rachel to the Planetarium."

"I know. I'll fill you in."

That Saturday, wanting to be better than prompt, I entered the gallery at three fifty and found Mr. and Mrs. Burns and their friends already there. The two women were looking at work in the section next to mine. I wondered which one was Jenny. The men were huddled together, closely examining and discussing *Number 10*. Their involvement was so intense, that they were startled by my greeting, like two little boys caught in a mischievous act.

"Ah, you are here! Bill, I'd like you to meet this remarkable artist."

Introductions were exchanged, with Mr. Carrington insisting in a deep bass voice, "Call me 'Bill'."

"This is quite a painting," he continued, "This *Number 10* of yours. Dan has been raving about it, and now I can see why. He tells me he's going to bid tor it. I'm sorry I didn't see it first."

"Thanks, Bill. I take that as a compliment."

Bill and Dan both laughed loudly.

Hearing the loud laughter, the women came from the other section to join us. The tall blonde led the way. She was introduced as May Carrington. Dan then introduced his wife, Jenny. They were both attractive women, but there were significant differences in their emotional expression. May was coldly scrutinizing, while Jenny gave me a warm smile and friendly eyes. Perhaps Dan's report that she found my photograph handsome might really be true. If so, I wondered how he felt about that, especially because of my race. I wondered what tension might be between them and how that might affect our relationship.

Jenny showed appropriate interest in *Number 10*, but did not seem to share her husband's obsession. May Carrington remained strangely aloof. Her clipped "H'lo" was not even a pretense of friendliness. As I was wondering how our mutual suspicions might affect any "family outing," Jenny spoke to ease the tension,

"Mark, I'm looking forward to meeting your wife and daughter. Dan has told me how impressed he was with their charm and beauty. I think he said your wife's name is Gracie?"

"Yes, and our daughter is Sarah. Do you and Dan have children?"

"We have two. Tommy is thirteen and Julie is eleven. How old is Sarah?"

"Sarah is nine. What about the Carringtons? Do they have children?" I had asked Jenny, because May had walked away, and the two men had gone aside to continue their confidential tete-a-tete.

"Yes, they have two teenagers: Beth, fourteen, and Marcia, sixteen. You'll meet them soon, ours and theirs."

"I'm looking forward to it. And I know Sarah will be glad that she and Julie are close in age."

Jenny was softening the tension that I felt with the others in the group. I believed that she and Gracie would like each other. As we talked, Dan approached, laughing his too-loud laugh.

"Ha-ha-ha! I knew it wouldn' take you two long to start getting chummy. Did you get my wife's phone number?"

Jenny and I ignored his insinuation. My guess was that she had long endured such behavior. While he might have hoped that I would take his comment as a joke, his annoyance was obvious. I was thankful when Dan finally announced that they should leave.

As if he had been waiting for this moment alone, Dan took an envelope from his pocket and handed it to me, grinning broadly as he did.

Opening the envelope, I found one of the pictures he had taken of *Number 10* and me.

"It came out rather well for an amateur like me, don't you think?"

"This doesn't look like the work of an amateur to me, Dan. It's a very good picture. And I remember that you shot your pictures with a classic camera."

"Well, it is a good camera. It's a Canon EOS A2E. Usually I use a digital, but I decided to use my old camera this time."

"I haven't really been in to cameras. I don't know much about that EOS A2E stuff."

"Ha-ha-ha. You don't really need that to take good pictures. That wouldn't help a bit if I didn't know how to aim the camera, hold it steady, and click the shutter at the right time. The real old pros, like Steichen and Van Derzee, could do it with just a simple box. None of the fancy stuff we have today."

Dan surprised me. Perhaps he was not so Philistine after all. He did have knowledge of the early masters of photographic art, even if he seemed to know nothing of other art expressions. Such contradictions made it easier for me to understand how he could be married to someone like Jenny, but I still had no reason to trust him.

Before the others returned, I put away the picture. We said our good-byes, confirming that we would see each other soon. Compliments were repeated.

As I watched them walk through the courtyard from the gallery's window walls, I reviewed my mental sketches of the group. There was Jenny with her glow of warmth; Bill, who had so carefully searched the details of my work, sharing with Dan questions unknown to me; and May, with her cool, level, scrutinizing gaze. And there was the evidence that Dan was not completely uncultivated. All this I would report to Gracie. I also made a mental catalogue of their appearances, as I anticipated that both Gracie and Sarah would be expecting a report.

Jenny apparently guessed that I would be watching them leave. She was the only one to look back and wave again. Although her height was only average, she had the figure and carriage of a fashion model. Her nearly waist-length dark brown hair wafted behind her in the gentle autumn breeze. The image of her blush-tinted mouth and her sparking gray-green eyes that spoke so eloquently, would stay with me. I could not deny the attraction, but obviously this would not be included in my report back to Gracie and Sarah. Gracie could still be confident that, for me, she would always be the most beautiful woman on earth.

May was taller than Jenny; attractive, but lacking in personal charm. Her blonde hair was closely page-boy coiffed around the deep tan which framed her mascara-lidded, cold blue eyes. I recalled from our closer contact, her scarlet lips drawn thin, matching the message in her piercing, searching look.

Bill was about the same height as Dan; not quite as broad shouldered, but better postured, in spite of being a little paunchy. He looked to be in his early fifties, with graying temple hair, a strong angular face, large ears and light gray eyes set deep under heavy, graying brows. I hadn't noticed his slight limp and extra long arms until I watched him walk through the courtyard.

After they were out of sight, I asked Cindy, the receptionist, if she had noted their time of arrival.

"They came in at three thirty. And those guys just hung around your *Number 10* until you got here. They sure seemed to have a lot to say about it. Maybe one of them will buy it."

Before I could respond, Cindy turned away to answer a viewer's question. I would not tell Cindy that I did not think either one of them was interested in the piece as an art work. It seemed that they knew something about it that I did not know. As I was anxiously questioning this possibility, Gracie and Sarah appeared. I moved quickly out the door to meet them, calling out "Good-bye" to Cindy.

Sarah ran to give me a hug and Gracie, already expecting a disappointing answer, asked, "Mark, have they gone already?"

Gracie was not surprised to hear that they had just missed them. They were both anxious to hear, however, my descriptions of their visit and my descriptions of them. Sarah was glad to learn that other children would be joining us, especially Julie, the Burns' eleven-year-old daughter.

At home, we all just collapsed – Gracie and I on the sofa, Sarah in her favorite armchair. Looking at Gracie and Sarah, I felt truly blessed to have them as my closest friends, confidantes and advisors. I was just beginning to feel relaxed when the phone rang. It was Cindy from the gallery.

"Mark, there's a couple here interested in buying your *Number 7*, and they want to know if the price is negotiable. They can't hear me now, so let me say that I have the sense that they can easily afford your price and more."

Number 7 celebrated the Caravan to Cuba, which defied the embargo imposing hardships on the Cuban people. Cindy was full of enthusiasm, but I doubted that the couple was serious. I let her know that my price was not negotiable, and asked her to call back if they were still interested.

Gracie went to fix supper, while Sarah showed me her purchases from the planetarium.

Although Cindy had not called, our doorbell rang, and I found a couple at the door, whom I recognized as the ones who had engaged Cindy's attention as I was leaving the gallery. They were a handsome pair, both casually dressed, in what looked to be limited production SoHo sportswear. They seemed to be in their early thirties. He was a blonde, Scandinavian type; she an Afro-Latin.

"It's Tim Bennett here, Mr. DeLouise," the man said. "And this is Rita Sanchez. We want to talk with you about buying a painting."

How had they gotten past security? I had thought I might go down to meet them if Cindy called, but I definitely had not wanted them in my home.

Anticipating the security concern, Tim explained, "We came in with Cindy, after she locked up the gallery. We came in the courtyard door. We hope you don't mind."

I did mind. Cindy meant well, but she needed to learn some things about dealing with potential buyers. I made an effort to be polite, although I was not optimistic about a sale. I tended to identify with other inter-racial couples, and I was not immune to Rita's smile.

"Please come in. Come on downstairs where we can discuss this in a more comfortable setting."

Gracie, curious to see our visitors, was waiting as we got to the lower level. I had invited our visitors to be seated, but Tim was too busy scanning the paintings on our walls and everything else in sight to hear me. Meanwhile, Rita expressed what seemed to be a genuine interest in my work; then made herself comfortable in a chair as she observed Tim's behavior.

"Tim, Mr. DeLouise is waiting."

"Oh, sorry. I just had to look at your paintings. They're really great. By the way, may we call you Mark?"

This concern over using first names was getting tiresome. Already I was associating him with the Carringtons and Burns. His aggressive scanning of our home was adding to my discomfort.

"Mark, I really like your *Number 7*. What a tribute to solidarity! But fifteen grand is more than I can handle. I assume you're open to negotiation. I'm prepared to give you ten."

"You can't be serious. That's cutting my price by a third. That's five thousand bucks you're talking about, and it would be a hardship to knock off even one. But I do have paintings I can let you have for ten if you're interested."

"Well, I'm only interested in *Number 7* right now. But can I look around some more? Maybe I'll see something I like almost as much that's in my price range."

Although still distrusting his motives, I was not going to deny his request. I invited Rita to help him pick something out.

Rita indicated her interest in my work, but did not seem to think she could influence his choice.

"I'd love to look at more of your work," she said, "but it's his money. Your paintings are powerful – they show the depths of good and evil."

"La lucha continua," I responded. "The struggle continues."

"In many languages. Your language is the language of paint."

Rita appreciated my "language", but had no money. Tim seemed to have an ulterior motive. I knew that he was looking at more than my paintings. If he had come to spy, what did he expect to find?

When they had finished their tour, they were both full of

compliments. Rita seemed sincere, but I had to wonder if Tim was somehow connected to Dan and Bill.

They thanked us for the tour and left. I had given them both my business card. Tim said that he would "definitely" keep in touch, but I did not believe him. And even though he never mentioned *Number 10*, I was sure that his visit was connected to this work. I watched his every move, but could not figure out what he was looking for.

On a certain level, I had envied Gracie for being too occupied to entertain our guests. But the kitchen where she worked was also her "listening post," which I knew she would use to her advantage. I needed to hear what she thought of our guests. Gracie declined my offer to help with dinner, but was ready to share her thoughts.

"Rita seemed o.k., but this guy Tim is scary. He definitely was not here to buy. I can't help but think that in some way he's connected to Dan and Bill, even though he never mentioned *Number 10*."

"I know. I think he just wanted to look around. If he expected us to believe that he was interested in *Number 7*, he must have thought we were idiots. His real interest is *Number 10*. But why? What do they know about *Number 10* that we don't know? Understandably, it attracts a lot of attention. They cannot know how it came to be painted, but they must know something about what it represents; something that I wish we knew."

"Maybe this will all become clear soon. But for now, let's eat. Dinner is ready. Tell Sarah to get ready while I put the food on."

Chapter 4

* ——————— ✦ ——————— *

AN OMINOUS APPEARANCE

I n our early years together, Gracie and I had no interest in church. We had both grown up in church-going families, but there had been nothing in either of our very different church experiences that drew us back. At best, we had known church as irrelevant, at worst a culture club. But we knew the role that Martin Luther King had played making real change. So when a friend invited us to his "different" church, we accepted and found it to be meaningful for us.

This Sunday we were going to church. Our pastor, Jim Daniels, knew how to take a difficult reading and make it relevant. His simple language was never an insult to the complex mind and often included stories that even a child could understand. We were surprised, however, when he chose one of the most difficult and abused texts for his focus:

> Fallen, fallen is Babylon the great! It has become a haunt of
> every foul spirit,
> a haunt of every foul bird, a haunt of every foul and hateful
> beast

As Jim continued with this reading from *Revelation* 18, I wondered not only how he would make sense of this for young people, but how he would relate it to some of our more "progressive" adults. In my growing up, such verses had often been used to blame victims for their own oppression.

But we knew this would not be Jim's tack. His identification of the USA with Babylon was clearly political. He brought this identification to still another level by an analogy with the dysfunctional human family. This was particularly useful to the several members of our congregation who worked in the mental health field. A serious dysfunction of the human family, he explained, is its worship of human authority. We are children of God, not children of the companies or institutions we work for; not children of the state, which only has its own interests in mind. When our hope for God's Kingdom becomes confused with the American dream, we are in great danger.

He described the world's dysfunction as chronicled daily in newspapers, heard on radio and seen on television. He put it all in a global family context, with the USA, as "super power" at the head of the family of nations. Pathologies of lesser powers frequently were manifestation of the "parent's" sickness. I was especially glad to be taping his sermon when he said,

"Beginning with our childhood, we are taught – at home and in school – to take pride in being American citizens. But as a child I was blessed with parents who taught me that being a good person has nothing to do with being the citizen of any nation, but everything to do with serving the will of God. This blessing enabled me as I grew older to become more and more aware of the complex nature of our dysfunction; the evil expressed, individually and corporately, throughout God's world."

Jim's pulpit style was commanding, no matter what his mood. To emphasize a point, he would pause, and lean his broad, tall six foot plus frame forward. His light brown complexion would redden with emotion. He would scan the congregation, making you feel that he had made eye contact with you, that he was preaching directly to you, calling you to account for allowing the "dysfunctional parent" to reign. He continued,

"We still hold the hope that someday the cruelties we inflict on ourselves and on each other, will come to an end. Today, as we prepare for a new millennium, we see that previously undreamed of technologies could make possible a world without material want. We could have the power to act as global community. God calls on us to make this happen.

"But other voices tell us it can never be. How naïve, they say, to have such hope. Do we not realize the profundity of the world's sin? Do we really believe that we can make a difference?"

Understandings among the listeners was probably mixed. The message was difficult for some, particularly children, but I did not see how he could make it any easier. Most in the congregation continued to keep rapt attention.

"God has given us a beautiful, bountiful home in which to live, and for which we must care. Some of us here are commendably conscientious in our personal efforts to recycle, and limit our use of fossil fuels. But unless we confront the greatest polluter and destroyer in all of history, the US military, we are doomed to certain extinction. Let's be clear. If we confuse loyalty to the state and to our prized culture with loyalty to God, we are truly dysfunctional.

"We have a choice. We can support a system that depends on the exploitation of the earth and the creatures that dwell on it (including our fellow humans), or we can find a system in which God's gifts are respected and shared. We can recruit armies and police to guard corporate wealth controlled by the few, or we can let the workers around the world who produce this wealth share control of the fruits of their labor. We can choose to walk the path of redemption, recognizing our sisters and brothers as part of our same human family, in co-creative partnership, or we can identify with the forces of oppression, believing that we alone are God's chosen, and that those who suffer, suffer because they are not more like us."

Jim's model of the dysfunctional family had helped bridge the gap between the apocalyptic imagination of the first century and the scientific mind that characterized our congregation. As performer/

preacher, he dramatized the symbolism of the text, but crafted his sermon in language that most of his congregation would understand.

In study group earlier this year, Jim had shown me how, at Christendom's inception, ruling class interests had used elements of Greek philosophy to spiritualize and de-politicize the scriptures. We had noted that Frederick Engels (a declared atheist) had written a response to the Book of Revelation. Although he lacked the tools of modern scholarship, he understood the essence of its revolutionary message.

As the sermon ended, I felt somewhat overwhelmed by Jim's righteous anger. It was our custom after a sermon to meet for discussion and ask questions. After our recent experiences, however, and my resulting emotional state, I was not ready to share my thoughts. As I wondered what Gracie's feelings were, I felt her pull at my jacket. She also wanted to leave.

So after thanking Jim for a powerful sermon, we headed after Sarah, whom we found at the snack and beverage table. She also was ready to leave, because her friends were not there.

As we moved toward the door, I could have sworn that I saw Tim Bennett quickly move across the room and turn toward the side exit. My attempt at pursuit was impeded by a friend who wanted to introduce me to her visiting sister, who was also an artist. So I never got to see if it was really him. But when Gracie told me that she also thought she had seen him, I knew that we both couldn't have been mistaken.

What was this man doing in our church on Sunday morning? Tim Bennett, whose visit to our house has raised such serious suspicions, had now just left our church. Clearly he had hoped that we would not see him before he left. Apparently he had come to further check us out and check out our congregation. His tracking us must have had something to do with *Number 10*, but what? On the way home, Gracie and I had difficulty carrying on a normal conversation. Sarah picked up our tension,

"Is something wrong? Are you guys alright?"

I had hoped that our anxiety would not be so obvious. I didn't know what to say. I was relieved when Gracie responded with,

"Jim has reminded us of all that needs to be done to change our world. I guess we're just trying to do some serious thinking. But we need to talk about it. And we all need to keep learning so that we can know what to do."

"Yes, I know it's serious. And scary. I've never seen Jim so angry."

"He was angry. I think he was trying to tell us we should all be angry about the way things are going in our world. If we all loved God and cared about each other, we wouldn't allow so many bad things to happen. Whether we're young or old, we can speak out when we know things are wrong. We need to learn from each other and work together."

I was thankful for Gracie's response, but not sure that Sarah was convinced that we didn't also have more immediate concerns.

When we got home there was a message on our phone from Dan Burns. I called him right back Next Sunday's museum date would be at 2 o'clock. Then he put Jennie on the line.

"Hi, Mark. I'm making a change in our dinner plans. We'd like you and your family to eat at our house instead of a restaurant. I hope that will work for you."

I felt better talking to Jenny. I thanked her and said we would be looking forward to the visit, which, of course, was not true. A home visit, however, was better than a restaurant and might even answer some of our questions.

"I promise to make something nice," Jenny added. "I cook healthy food. Dan says that's not important for him, but I usually try to fix food that's healthy and tasty – for me and him."

We confirmed the details of the plan and said good-bye. Gracie was pleased to hear of the change.

"This will give us a chance to see where and how these folks live," I observed. "Maybe get some insights into the feelings we have about Dan."

"What feelings, Dad?"

Sarah had been busy thumbing through a magazine as we talked.

Her question caught me off guard, because I hadn't realized that she had been listening. Gracie again came to the rescue.

"Dan Burns might want one of your Dad's paintings. He may be getting chummy because he's trying to buy it for less than it's worth. Maybe Sunday will prove us wrong."

I was thankful that Gracie made this attempt to hide our worries from Sarah, but I was uncomfortable with the deception. We ourselves were still trying to figure out the truth. We feared the truth and feared that all of us would soon enough have to know it. The appearance of Tim Bennett in church had just compounded our concern.

Sarah continued silently thumbing through the magazine. I was sure that she hadn't believed her mother – not now or when her mother tried to cover our anxieties before. The look in Gracie's eyes echoed my perception. Shifting focus, Gracie announced,

"I could use some help in the kitchen, Sarah. Mark, you can set the table."

Chapter 5

* ———— ⊛ ———— *

THE FAMILY OUTING

On the awaited "family outing" Sunday, we did not bother to go home after church. We were due at the museum at two, so we stayed at church to talk with friends and enjoy the coffee-hour snacks. When we arrived uptown we were lucky to find parking close to the entrance. The Burns and the Carringtons arrived minutes later. Dan immediately began to make introductions. Since he knew everyone, I was able to overlook his grandiose manner of taking charge.

"Gracie and Sarah, this is my wife, Jenny, who Mark has already met. And these are our children, Tommy and Julie. I would also like you to meet my good friends, Bill and May Carrington. Mark has met them, but not their beautiful daughters, Beth and Marcia."

The introductions felt a bit awkward, until Jenny spoke up.

"Hi, Gracie and Sarah. I've been looking forward to meeting you. Now I can see for myself what Dan has been raving about."

"Hi, Jenny. Sarah and I have heard great things about you, too. It's good to meet you."

Sarah smiled and said "Hello" to Jenny. Her charm worked instantly with the other children, who had given only polite acknowledgment of our adult presence. Bill glowered when introduced to Gracie. He appeared unpleasantly surprised that Gracie was white. Dan, perhaps for his own amusement, had not told him what to expect.

May scrutinized Gracie as she had me at Westbeth Gallery. All she said when introduced was, "Hi."

We found our way to Jacob Lawrence's instantly recognizable work. A prominent biographical statement plus descriptive notes posted at each piece, made any docent role I might have played unnecessary. I noted where the interests of our group were focused. The kids liked his *Pool Parlor* and *Dancing at the Savoy*, both of which expressed competitive recreation. I noted the interweavings of ethos and pathos in these and other Lawrence works. The Savoy dancers, for example, clearly formed a close, protective and unifying circle, while a small group of white spectators sat off in a corner. The immediate impression of gaiety was contradicted by racial tension.

Street Clinic caught Gracie and Jenny's attention. Perhaps a shared feeling of compassion drew them to the lines of waiting sufferers.

Dan, Bill and May remained a triumvirate. They spent time looking at and discussing *Race Riots*, *The Rebels*, and *Migrants Held at Railroad*, from his *Migration of the Negro* series. They were especially interested in *Migrants Held at Railroad*, depicting a white policeman blocking a door through which black migrants were attempting to pass. My uneasy reaction to their focus kept coming back to me as we moved on to other areas of the exhibit. I had flash-backs to Dan's and Bill's intense conversations responding to my own *Number 10*. This time May was part of their chemistry.

As we prepared to leave the museum, the children talked excitedly, while Jenny, Gracie and I shared our insights. Then we heard Dan's loud,

"Well, what did you all think of Jacob Lawrence? Pretty damn powerful, wouldn't you say?"

The kids responded with conventional affirmations, dampened by Dan's overbearing presence.

Then Sarah came to me and confided, "The paintings are interesting. But not as powerful as yours."

Dan overheard and added, "I know you're not saying that because he's your dad, Sarah. I agree with you one hundred per cent. What did you think of the show, Mark?"

Ignoring his fake enthusiasm for both my paintings and Jacob's, I tried to put our works in perspective. "Jake and I just do what we do. It's not a competition. We paint from our own very personal view, with the hope that people will understand the human struggles we express."

"Well said, Mark! Well said! Now let's all go and have something to eat at the Burns' house."

His remark needed only an accompanying pat on my head, to dramatize his paternalistic bluster. The glances exchanged between Bill and May seemed to magnify his counterfeit words and manner. Jenny, meanwhile, was busy exploring the contents of her purse, an exercise which seemed to have no purpose other than covering her embarrassment.

On our way to the car, I wondered about Sarah's impressions of the conversations. I knew that Gracie had been paying close attention and figured that she probably knew my thoughts, but I didn't feel ready to discuss any of this now. Although we all must have had questions, we were letting them wait as we quietly primed ourselves for a sure-to-be curious visit to the Burns' house.

The Burns lived in a luxury condo on East 72nd Street. They had made available a parking space for us, so we had only to give the attendant our ticket, park our car and head for their apartment, number 37B. Dan greeted us at the door. "Well, here you are! Come right in and make yourselves at home."

Jenny then appeared, greeting us with a radiant smile. "Welcome – Mark, Gracie and Sarah. It's so good to have you join us."

Jenny led us into the living room, where the Carringtons had already claimed the two most comfortable chairs. Bill nodded and said, "Hi," but May just nodded and tried to fake a smile. Dan came right behind us, shouting,

"Alright, folks. How about drinks before dinner! What'll y' have?"

Dan offered a range of choices. Gracie and I chose Burgundy, which I would nurse through dinner, since I would be driving. The food was delicious, and varied to please diverse palates, including the vegetarian. It was followed with a refreshingly not-too-sweet peach cobbler and rum raisin ice cream. Conversation was a superficial potpourri of current events, personal origins, art and, on a more challenging level, science fiction. It was Dan and Jenny's son, Tommy, who instigated this intergenerational topic. Tommy, a serious Trekky, asked if we believed in flying saucers. I assumed that the question was really for us, as he was probably already much too aware of the negative attitudes of his family and the Carringtons. Still, we were hoping that someone else would respond. Finally, Dan, seemingly embarrassed by the question, said sternly,

"You know my thinking on that subject, Thomas."

Jenny fended for her son with a gentle, "Dan!"

Wanting to give Tommy further support, I simply said, "Tommy, there are many possibilities in this mysterious universe. I don't think all of those people who reported sightings were necessarily mistaken. Some were even U.S. Air Force pilots."

On that note, Gracie and Sarah seemed relieved, while Jenny smiled in my direction. Tommy and the other kids looked up approvingly. But Bill and May turned expectantly toward Dan, waiting for him to speak. Dan forced a smile and quickly terminated Tommy's topic.

"Well, nothing follows dessert better than relaxation. Let's leave the table to our maid, Emma, and take our drinks back to the living room. Maybe you kids would like to check out our recreation room."

While I welcomed Dan's initiative, I felt no less anxious. As we adults returned to the living room, Dan turned our conversation to the Westbeth show, and *Number 10* was quickly given center stage. Dan proudly displayed the picture he had taken of me standing next to it on opening night. Of course everyone had already seen the picture. It was just his way of setting things up for what was to follow. Dan could not be bothered with any more intergenerational conversation when his real concern related to *Number 10*. I didn't understand it then, but I was to learn later that the seemingly usual questions about my style, subject and message that he and Bill asked, had a specific, and for me, dangerous intent.

Chapter 6

THE UNMASKING

It was at the closing of the show three weeks later that Dan quietly and privately identified himself to me as FBI Agent Burns. He informed me that *Number 10* would be confiscated because it was an exact representation of the workings of a top secret U.S. government facility Among all my fantasies and fears, nothing had come close to this. Of course, Gracie and I had suspected Burns of something, but we knew not what. And because of this, I had hoped that we might find out "what" from our observation of him. But we had learned nothing. And what Dan was telling us now made no sense. It was too incredible.

Although Dan's interest and the attention of the Carringtons and probably Tim Bennett had been serious concerns, I never suspected that I might have done anything illegal. The jolt of this accusation brought on a great wave of fear. What kind of trouble was I in?

Number 10 had been produced by the "force," with my coerced assistance. If it's complicated structure really was top secret, why had I been directed to paint it? I could have explained the UFO connection to the feds, but I was afraid to reveal it. The truth might only make things worse. They would not believe me and would most likely use such a story against me. Unless the extraterrestrials who got me into this mess would back me up, my defense would be useless. I needed extraterrestrial help.

Dan continued, "Mark, it looks like we're dealing with an espionage case here. You are going to have to answer some very serious questions. But right now, my partner, Allen Symes, will help you take your other paintings up to your studio. I'll stay here with *Number 10*. That goes up last, and then we'll talk."

"You do not understand how I came to make this painting," I managed to say calmly. "I do not understand it myself, but I can say that I definitely know nothing about any secret government building. Obviously, if I had felt that I had something to hide, I would not have exhibited my work publicly."

I was trying to appear cool. I could not let Dan see how terrified I was.

"Well, Mark, there had to be some kind of espionage by somebody for you to come up with this structure."

I was feeling an increasing sense of rage. I dared not open my mouth. An acrid mix of disbelief, resentment and confusion stirred within me. Why had I been made to do this painting?"

Allen Symes, presumably Agent Symes, had been busily examining *Number 10*. I had noticed Symes earlier in the evening, even then focusing on *Number 10*. I had thought it unusual, since most of the other black visitors had shown more interest in my paintings dealing with racial themes. So I was not surprised to learn who he was. After Dan introduced us, Symes and I returned all the other paintings to my studio. Then the three of us started out of the gallery with *Number 10*. Our gallery receptionist, Cindy, had not been close enough to hear what we were saying. Assuming that I had sold *Number 10*, she gave me a thumbs-up sign. I answered with a thumbs-down and said that I would call.

We were in my apartment for only two or three minutes when we heard the intercom buzz. It was Bill Carrington. Dan went to the door, leaving Allen and me to begin wrapping *Number 10* with black plastic. Bill and Dan spent a few minutes in private conversation before coming down to the studio. They kept their voices low until they started down the steps, with Bill's base voice booming,

"It doesn't look good, Dan. It doesn't look good."

Carrington was now re-introduced as Colonel William F. Carrington. No longer jovial and sociable, he aggressively and sternly asked,

"Well, Mark, what's this all about? What've you got against America?"

"What have I got against America, Colonel? Nothing that would lead me to espionage. I am an artist, who puts on canvas my aesthetic inspiration. I don't know and would never think of trying to know about any secret military facility. I love America enough, as my paintings show, to try and change it. I call for peace and justice and more equitable sharing of wealth and power. My grounding is spiritual. *Number 10* is obviously not like my other paintings. But I swear that its image just came to my imagination. It is nothing I ever actually saw, not even in a photograph or drawing. I was just called to paint it. If you're saying that it really exists, I have no idea where or why."

The two men looked at each other. Obviously, they did not believe me. My mind raced ahead to what I could tell Gracie and Sarah if I were arrested. Dan spelled out their next steps,

"All we need now is the painting. We want to study it very carefully, to make sure it's what we believe it is. In the meantime, I would advise you to stay close to home and get yourself a damn good lawyer."

After they left with the painting I realized that my fear of immediate arrest was not rational. To arrest me they needed more indictable evidence. And in order to gather more evidence, they needed to survey my activities and contacts. Now they needed my "freedom." I assumed that our phone was being tapped, our email monitored and our car and home bugged. I was probably being followed whenever I left the house. Dan had to know that I could never have gained access to this well-secured building. The feds had to assume that someone on the inside was the master spy. This spy must have somehow transmitted the closely guarded image to me. But, since the image would most likely have been a digital photograph, for transmission to others in this supposed plot, why would a painting be needed? How, in fact, could a publicly exhibited painting serve any anti-government interest?

Chapter 7

TIME FOR COUNSEL

As I speculated on how these government agents might be thinking, I wondered how Gracie and I could possibly have thought that we could figure out their motives. The efforts we had made to observe them now seemed childish. It was as if we had been trying to pretend that our suspicions could be overcome by going along with Dan's charade.

Why had the painting intruded into my life? Why had the feds claimed that it depicted a "top secret" government facility. I had no credible explanation that might help me escape from this situation. Perhaps the painting's intricately complex technical details suggested military use, and Burns and Carrington, driven by patriotic zeal, assumed that it depicted a real, but secret, U.S. military facility. Perhaps, I feared, they were right. But how could this be? And why? Why would the "force" want me to paint and exhibit a secret building? Was it part of some plan for confrontation? Didn't I have a right to know? I fantasized that the little orb might come by with answers to my questions, but instead I was left in ignorance. Soon I heard Gracie at the door.

"I thought you had company," Gracie said, in a tone of surprise. "I see they left. I stopped by the gallery, thinking you might still be there, but Cindy said that Dan and some other guy helped you bring your work upstairs. Who was the other guy?"

"The other guy." I paused before I went on to tell Gracie much more than she was prepared to hear. "It's not just who the other guy is; it's who Burns and Carrington really are.

"Burns is Agent Burns. FBI. And the other guy is his partner, Allen Symes. Carrington came up a few minutes later. Colonel William F. Carrington."

It took Gracie awhile to respond. She had shared my ill-defined fears, but now we could think of no possible scenarios to quell these fears. "This is beyond any of my imaginings," she said. "I know this is about *Number 10*, but why? What is this worry about *Number 10*?"

"According to Dan, the structure depicted in *Number 10* is a top-secret U.S. government building. Dan and the others took the painting with them. To 'study it very carefully,' he said, because they think they have an espionage case. He told me to stay close to home and get myself a 'damn good lawyer.'"

"Call Leslie right away, Mark."

"Right away," I repeated. Thank God we knew an excellent lawyer. I had already planned to call this lawyer, Leslie Chen, who was not only very competent, but our friend. I picked up the phone and dialed.

Leslie had been to the show's opening and, of course, remembered the painting. I told her briefly what had happened. She seemed to understand the seriousness of my situation

"I need to get your story as soon as possible. My home is more private than my office. Can you both come by tomorrow evening at seven?"

We thanked Leslie and confirmed the date and then adjusted our schedule for the visit. Sarah would again sleep over with her friend Rachel, in case we needed to stay late at Leslie's.

We approached Leslie's home the next evening with anxiety. Although we had confidence in her ability, we wondered if she would believe my story.

She greeted us warmly at the door. "Come on in, you two. Make yourselves comfortable. I've got hot tea or coffee. And ginger cookies that I baked myself."

She seemed to sense that we needed to ease into the heavy stuff. Her conversation began with inquiries about mutual friends. She seemed to be testing our emotional tone; then moving slowly into the purpose of our visit.

"I know this is very scary for you both, but you can count on me to put my best efforts into trying to clear this up. For now, try to relax, because I'm just going to start with some procedural questions. We need dates, times, places, conversations, witnesses. If you've forgotten something, Mark, just say so, and Gracie, if you remember something that Mark isn't clear about, speak up. You're going to be asked a lot of questions. Your answers will need to be straight and consistent. Tell me everything. I'll decide what to use, and when and how."

Leslie's almond eyes widened as she waited for my response. I was lucky to have her as my lawyer. Gracie gave me a gentle nudge to begin.

"I hear you, loud and clear. What I am going to tell you will be hard to believe, but everything will be the truth. But before I start, I have to ask you a question which may seem strange. Strange, but believe me, relevant. It's about UFO's: Do you believe people have actually encountered them?"

"Well, I never have. But I'm open to the possibility. How does this relate to *Number 10?*"

"We'll explain. This has to come before any procedural questions."

Leslie nodded consent and waited for me to begin. It was as if she was not surprised by my UFO question.

I told her basically everything, but, of course, it was only a summary. The UFO sighting, the painting which I did not control, our contacts with Dan Burns and Bill Carrington and their families; the visit of Tim Bennett and Rita Sanchez and Tim's appearance at our church; the revelation of Dan Burns as FBI agent and Bill Carrington as colonel, and their confiscation of *Number 10*. Gracie corroborated.

Leslie had let us talk without interruption. "Amazing," she said when I had finished. "If I didn't know you, I might not believe you. But you two are among the sanest and most honest people I know. The feds, however, won't buy this. I'm assuming that they are looking for your links to someone inside this mystery building. They won't find anyone, but they'll continue to keep you under close surveillance. They most likely think that you will lead them to someone or something else. You can be sure that they've already done a thorough background check on both of you, especially you, Mark."

"I'm afraid I was wrong telling Dan Burns that the painting was created from my imagination."

"Let's not think of it as right or wrong, Mark. You felt under pressure to tell him something, and you knew the truth wouldn't work, in spite of the fact that it's the only explanation that makes sense. Apparently, your E.T friends came here well equipped – electromagnetically, telepathically, and with whatever else in super advanced technology they need to check us out. We might assume that they have observed us for quite some time, and made a careful study of our warring ways. If this is true (incredible as it seems), they would be particularly interested in the locations of our military hardware and its control center. Perhaps a wise security measure."

Leslie had just given shape to my ill-defined speculations. I had been so personally involved with this extraterrestrial power, that I had found it difficult to articulate what made sense to Leslie and now made sense to me. Gracie also appreciated Leslie's theory.

"It makes sense," Gracie said, "that they might be concerned about our world's escalating destructive power. But how do we fit into this?"

"That's the big question," I said. Why did they pick *me* to produce this work and how might it serve their purpose? My family and I don't need this trouble."

"Perhaps you were chosen," Leslie responded, "because you are one of the few trustworthy earthlings. Being chosen was never meant to be easy. Perhaps they needed an artist who understood the responsibility for raising political consciousness. I have no idea how the painting might serve their purpose, but it seems that it must."

"They could have chosen someone else."

"You may not be the only one, Mark. We don't know, do we?"

"No, we don't, but I would certainly feel better if I knew there were others." If this is really supposed to be a salvific endeavor, we would need a community of artists in supportive contact, sharing insights on Close Encounters."

"Who knows? It might come to that. But for now, you have me and Gracie." Leslie paused. "Now what about Sarah? What does she know?"

"We didn't want to burden her mind with too much," Gracie answered. "But Mark and I have been having second thoughts. She needs to hear the facts from her parents before she hears some TV version. She'll need to know what to say when her friends ask her questions."

Leslie nodded. That was one thing she would not have to convince us of. "I have enough information for tonight," she concluded. We didn't do much with procedural questions, did we? The important thing now is to let me know everything that develops."

As we left, I thought about Leslie's reference to me as "chosen." Gracie had used those same words when we first shared the sighting. It sounded a bit grandiose. Still, this contact seemed so important that I should not allow myself to be afraid.

Chapter 8

* ———— ✦ ———— *

THE LITTLE ORB CONFIRMS

S arah had known all along that something wasn't right. As we sat down for our "things-we-need-to-tell-you" talk, she responded with an "it's-about-time" expression. The talk was long overdue. She had to hear us now before the situation became more serious, before the possibility of my being hauled off to jail became real. We carefully went over the details of our situation, assuring her that we were confident of a victorious outcome, in spite of early setbacks we might have. This was a family secret, not even to be shared with her best friend Rachel. Sarah listened attentively and asked appropriate questions, showing particular interest when I told her about what we assumed to be an extraterrestrial role in the production of *Number 10*.

Since Sarah had never believed my explanation for *Number 10*, what I told her now made more sense to her. She expressed faith that the "force" would defend me against anything the feds might do. And while we hoped and prayed that she was right, we feared that there would be difficult times ahead. We felt that we had to prepare her.

"We believe that the E.T.'s have a positive plan," I said, "but we still have to deal with the feds. I don't think it's going to be easy. We are all going to have to be strong and have faith that things will work out eventually."

That night, while Gracie was sound asleep; my tossing and turning was halted by the sight of the little Orb floating over me. As I watched, it began sending me a telepathic message, assuring me that my family and I would get through this. I was then told that not only my family and I, but everyone who played a part in the *Number 10* drama, had been and continued to be, under close observation by the "force." Now the little Orb revealed that Gracie and I had been under FBI surveillance since the day after the opening of the exhibit, when Dan Burns first saw *Number 10*. My perception that Tim Bennett was also FBI was confirmed. He had come to our apartment pretending to be interested in buying a painting, but as Gracie had also guessed, he had just been there to check things out.

Now we knew why. This was his opportunity to plan re-entry when we were not at home. That opportunity was arranged by Dan Burns, who had gotten us to join him and his family and friends at the museum, followed by dinner. This gave Tim plenty of time to look for "evidence" and install bugging devices. His entry was done with a search warrant, and the cooperation of Fran Lynd, the building manager, who had been sworn to secrecy. I also learned from the Orb exactly where the bugs were and was warned against interfering with them in any way. I was advised to continue conversing normally and freely at home, in the car, and elsewhere, except when discussing confidential matters relating to the anticipated espionage case. In such matters, statements and questions were to be written, and exchanged for response.

Chapter 9

THE ARREST

T he story of the little Orb's visit and its monitoring of our situation had to be shared – first with Gracie and Sarah, and eventually with Leslie. For Gracie, as for me, it re-established our confidence in the power of the "force" and its caring for us. For Sarah, it was a validation of her insights independent of the adult world and a new sense of responsibility that comes with such insight.

This communication, of course, had to be written In anticipation of more such silent "dialogues," we decided to practice the activity, imagining future "conversations" with Leslie, as well as ourselves. As we gained proficiency in the process, it even turned out to be fun, especially for Sarah, whose "game" orientation helped to relieve at least some of our stress. We were, in this small way, putting one over on the FBI.

It was amusing to picture federal agents, waiting patiently to hear incriminating words, by way of their surveillance technology. They needed to confirm that *Number 10* was evidence of espionage in order to indict me. Most specifically, they hoped that I would identify a person within the secret facility whom they assumed to be the source of the image. Since, however, our "visitors-from-outer-space" were the source of the image, my painting had nothing to do with espionage. Any conversations relating to this might actually have proven my innocence if they could have been credible to the FBI mind. But since they could not, we assumed they would only hurt us. The feds might twist them into some nefarious meaning. We believed it best to follow the little Orb's advice.

Even though we could win this "game," we knew that the feds would not just disappear. And even without evidence that could make their charges stick, they would most probably be compelled to bring me in. When that happened, they would probe relentlessly to find my link within the government project. I did not, however, have the answers they wanted to hear, and they would not believe the truth. To tell them how I really came to do the painting would be an insult to their cool, defiant, personas and a challenge to their patriotism. They were not ready for truth.

Two weeks later, the little Orb sent another message. I would be arrested soon. Although they had no real evidence for an indictment, they would claim that allowing my continued freedom posed a serious danger to the state. On Monday morning, when Sarah and Gracie would both be at their schools and I would be home preparing for my job, I should expect that Dan Burns and Allen Symes would come to take me away. Their surveillance would already have informed them of our schedule. I believe that Dan chose this time because he wanted to avoid a confrontation with my family. Later he would have to inform them, because of course he would not know that they already knew.

When Sarah and Gracie left that morning, they did not know when they would see me again. Our parting communication included extra hugs and my assuring scribble that, "the 'force' is with us."

At about 9:30 that morning, Dan Burns called to say that he and his partner were on their way to "see" me. I wrote Gracie a note, again reassuring her of my faith and saying how much I loved them both. I knew that Gracie would be in touch with Leslie, and mentioned that as well.

Dan and Allen didn't come as grim-faced G-men. When I opened the door, I was surprised to see them almost smiling. I knew, however, that the smiles, which quickly disappeared, were not for me. Perhaps they had been sharing some humor on the way to our apartment. Except for a polite exchange of greetings at the door, no one spoke as we walked down the stairs to the living room, where they refused my offer of seats. Then, without hesitation, Agent Burns stated the purpose for their visit.

"Mark, I'm sorry to say, the time has come."

And placing his hand gently at first, then firmly on my shoulder, he continued almost apologetically,

"Mark DeLouise, I'm going to have to hold you on suspicion of conspiracy to commit espionage against the United States."

As if picking up the ambivalence in Dan's tone and informal language, Agent Symes looked at him questioningly. Then he returned to the task at hand and read me my Miranda rights.

Much to my surprise, Dan said that I would not be handcuffed. From the look on his face, Symes also was surprised.

"We're going out the West Street exit, to avoid drawing attention," Dan instructed.

Since I was not handcuffed, our exit probably would not have drawn attention. Still, I was relieved that I would encounter few, if any, of my neighbors on this route. I also realized that the FBI might have its own reasons for avoiding publicity at this time. After all, they did not have the connecting evidence to *Number 10* on which to base a case. They most likely hoped that interrogation would produce such evidence. It was going to be rough.

Their expectation was that I would eventually "confess" and there would be a big story to report. In the meantime, Dan was not eager for a "Free Mark DeLouise" movement. He was well aware that I had a loyal following in both the progressive and the artistic communities.

How long the secret of my incarceration could be maintained, however, depended on how Gracie and Leslie chose to deal with my incarceration. Gracie might be torn between the need to start organizing my support and the need to protect Sarah from the harassment of those who believed the charge against me. She probably would follow Leslie's advice. All I could do was pray.

As Agent Burns drove downtown, I noticed that we were on

Varick Street; and, not knowing where the federal "jail house" was, I asked where we were going. Agent Symes, who sat next to me in the back seat, responded.

"The Metropolitan Correctional Center is on Park Row, Mr. DeLouise. We're almost there."

Thoughts of being booked, fingerprinted, photo-mugged, and slammed behind bars in a cold drab cell raced through my head. I would be locked away from Gracie and Sarah for God knows how long. It certainly didn't help to hear Agent Burns say,

"Mark, we're here. I'm going to drive around to the back entrance to avoid the prying media. Allen, you can put the cuffs on now. We don't want this guy getting' away from us."

Their shared laughter suggested the insecurity they must have felt in their action. In spite of their diligent efforts, they still did not have a case. Burns' reference to my "getting away," was really his fear that they would never get the evidence to convict.

Chapter 10

———◉———

LOCK-UP

After the booking was complete, I exercised my right to call Gracie. Although I had left her a note, I needed to hear her voice and let her hear mine, find out what Sarah was doing and tell her where I was. Gracie reported that Leslie already knew where I was being held and was getting right to work. She assured me that Sarah was keeping faith, but I knew that that had to be difficult, in spite of the confidence she had expressed when I was still free. However any of us might feel, we weren't going to let each other hear anything in our voices but strength and hope. Tears would be held in reserve for joy when finally I would be vindicated. We all had to keep that faith.

In spite of my resolve to remain undaunted, as soon as the prison door slammed shut, thoughts of my risk surfaced. If I were found guilty, I could be sentenced to death. I prayed that the extraterrestrials had a sure plan.

The E.T.'s certainly had powers that my jailers did not have. I should not fear. I did have faith that they would assure my vindication, but when? In the meantime, I worried about the suffering of my family. What would be the reactions of Gracie's friends and colleagues? And how would Sarah's classmates and teachers respond? I did not think that Rachel and her family would believe the charges, but others might. I knew about the espionage trial of Julius and Ethel Rosenberg in the early 50's. My reading on that case had convinced me of their innocence, but still, they were executed. Their children were supported, but certainly suffered.

Standing in the middle of my cell with its loathsomely exposed toilet, I folded my arms and stared angrily at the bars that held me captive. Summoned undoubtedly by the emication of my thoughts, the little Orb appeared. Hovering over my head, it announced that I would be telepathically liberated, so that I could speak with Gracie. To facilitate this process, at least at first, I might have to lie down and relax.

I did not wait. Lying down on my cot, I closed my eyes and made an effort to calm myself. Soon I could not only see Gracie, but it was evident that she could see me. Our telesthesian images responded excitedly. We first assured each other that so far things were going as well as could be expected. Sarah was o.k., but we worried about the impact of more serious developments. Gracie would continue to keep Sarah informed, help her to understand, and support her faith.

Then Gracie's eyes signaled a surprise. "Mark, guess who we got a letter of support from today?"

Gracie went on to tell me that Jenny Burns had written to her. Her letter explained that when Dan told her everything, including his plan to arrest me, she knew that our phone was tapped, so calling was definitely out of the question. Gracie said that her letter had been mailed in a Network Life Insurance Company envelope; a business in which Jenny had a management position. She knew that since we were already on their marketing list, the FBI would not bother to check the envelope.

"You know that we usually just toss those things out, Mark, but somehow I just had to open this one."

"Of course you did. Don't you know why? It's the 'force,' Gracie – the same powerful entity that brought *Number 10* into our lives and is making it possible for us to be with each other telepathically right now. Doesn't that make sense?"

"Well, yeah, it does. I hadn't thought of it that way before, I guess because I haven't had the direct involvement with the 'force,' as we call it, that you have. Anyway, Jenny knows nothing about our mysterious ally, so even sending the letter the way she did was quite a risk."

"And the fact that she took such a risk really proves her sincerity, and how right we were to trust her. What else did she say?"

"She knew nothing about Dan's suspicions and his plan to use the museum trip and dinner engagement as an investigative set-up. She was shocked and confused by Dan's explanation that you had done a painting of a secret defense facility, because she knew you would not have been able to get in the building, and even if you had somehow received the picture, why would you want to display it publicly if you were involved in espionage? Jenny is in a difficult position, but she wants to help. She ended by expressing her concern about Sarah."

"Jenny took a real risk sending you that letter," I responded. "She is a brave friend."

At this point, we lost our telesthesic connection, but I no longer felt alone.

Chapter 11

※ ———————⬤———————— ※

A VISIT TO *NUMBER 10*

L ocked up, yet free – telepathically free to be with Gracie. How could I not feel empowered, even within the drab confines of my cell? Believing that, with the help of the little Orb, I could look forward to more "escapes," I felt hopeful, and, as if to reinforce my hope, the little Orb appeared again. Now it seemed to stay on stand-by, immediately responding to my pressing concerns. It had come to tell me that the telepathic channel shared by Gracie and me, would be permanently available for ours and Sarah's use, as long as I was imprisoned. He further added that, since Leslie's council was so important, she also would be included in this privilege.

But even with this assurance, I had trouble relaxing and getting to sleep. Anticipating the time when the story of my arrest became public, I anguished over the hardships for Gracie and Sarah. As these nightmarish thoughts continued, I began to feel sensations of my own movement. Involuntarily, I was up and walking on air. In this dream-like state, I was greeted by the little Orb.

"Follow me," the Orb instructed.

Obediently, I followed, and soon found myself in an environment I immediately recognized. It was the interior of the building in *Number 10*. As I entered further into this labyrinth, I was told to focus carefully on every intricate detail: the wirings, gauges, meters, dials, pipes, valves, levers, switches, alarms, computers, robots, clocks, intercoms, maps, charts, radios, cameras, etc. We then passed through a door without its having to be opened, down a flight of stairs, and into a corridor, where there was another door marked "GNS Control." My guide read "GNS" as Global Nuclear Silos." We passed through this closed door as we had the first.

There I saw an enclosed vehicle, suspended from an overhead track. As non-material presence, we entered the vehicle, which then moved on its track to the center of a circular area. On board were four men, a command staff monitoring a systems operation and workers below and around them. One-way glass allowed the command to observe the operation without being seen. Communications were radioed between command and workers. Of course, no one was aware of us.

We then moved into the operations area itself, through a door, down to a lower level, and into a well-fortified vault housing a walled safe. I was able to see clearly through its thick metal door. Here was a mechanism, my guide explained, to which only the President and a few secret men of power had access. This was the mechanism that controlled the release of nuclear missiles from the nation's silos.

Then, suddenly I was back in my physical body again, sitting on my prison cot, with the little Orb still hovering over my head. Its telepathic message was brief and reassuring.

"Remember every detail of all that you have seen, but tell no one until we advise you to do so. Do not worry. Do not worry about your family, yourself, or anything. Trust in us as we trust in you."

This was the first time I had heard the "force" referred to as "us" and "we." The little Orb had heretofore just come to deliver messages and instructions, leaving the nature of whom or what it represented open to my imagination. I still knew nothing about the "force" or why those representing it had needed me to paint this nuclear control center. Of course, I knew that our nation was prepared to deploy weapons of mass destruction. But now I had been chosen to see their facility, and now I knew what I had painted as *Number* 10. To what might all this lead, and what was my responsibility?

I wondered about those who had sent this little Orb. I tried to imagine what kind of persons or creatures they might be. On a mundane level, I wondered what they might wear, what they ate, how might they enjoy music, dance, and sex? What did they understand about God? How did they know of our nuclear weapons, and why was I involved?

I recalled movies I had seen, depicting interplanetary invasions of Earth. I had always believed that the most threatening of such films were promoted to raise mass anxiety, in order to give those who claimed to "protect," the power to rule. My real fear, however, was my own government with its potential for initiating nuclear annihilation.

"Trust in us, as we trust in you," the little Orb had said. Although I was yet to meet the little Orb's "people," somehow I felt a spiritual connection with whom I imagined them to be. My faith was in a new dimension. That night, I slept a deep and restful sleep.

The next morning, I was awakened by the jingling of keys, the sliding of heavy lock bolts, and growled commands rousing inmates. While other prisoners were being ordered to the mess hall, I was kept in isolation. A guard brought breakfast to my cell – orange juice, lukewarm coffee, white toast, and a bowl of cold gluey oatmeal. I could eat very little.

As the day went on, I listened to the rough voices of angry men, both guards and prisoners, the clatter of equipment being moved in the cell block, and, since my cell was not far from the office, telephones and office machines and more regulated voices. It was hard for me to imagine that my de-materialized self had just traveled to a secret military command center. I needed to involve myself in something other than these thoughts. I would try to get someone to bring me a book, but for now I distracted myself with a few exercises, physical and mental, and the hope of going home. I assumed that Gracie had called my job, and wondered what she had told them. They had to know that I wouldn't be coming in. While puzzling over this job communication, a guard appeared, turning his key in my cell lock.

Chapter 12

A QUESTIONABLE CASE

"**Y**our lawyer's here," the guard said in the disdainful tone of a man who believed he was addressing the worst of criminals. He couldn't have known of my spy status, so I didn't know what might have brought on this hostility. Nevertheless, in spite of his hateful tone, his announcement of Leslie's arrival was music to my ears.

I was led to a small room where Leslie was waiting. I could tell that the room had a one-way mirror, violating my right to attorney/client confidentiality. Leslie's "chin-up" smile did not cover her sadness at seeing me prisoner. My face, too, must have reflected the contradictions I felt – joy at seeing her, but feeling the hardship of my situation. Her strong lawyerly countenance was reassuring.

With an exchange of looks, Leslie and I celebrated the knowledge that we could be in telepathic communication. For our purposes of communication, her visit was not even necessary, but it was important to normalize appearances, and I welcomed her physical presence. Although we believed that we were being observed and listened to, our telepathic powers made it unnecessary to demand another room. Changing rooms would offer no guarantee that we would not be bugged, so rather than make an issue of the room, we pretended that we did not notice. That decision and all our secret planning were done telepathically, while we carried on an irrelevant audible discussion designed to frustrate their unlawful surveillance.

If they were listening, it was good for them to hear Leslie say, "Mark, this shouldn't be happening to you. You and Gracie are two of this country's best citizens. I know there are things you'd like to see changed; changes that many loyal Americans seek. But what you've been accused of would never be your way of trying to bring about change. Because I believe that so strongly, I'm taking your case pro bono. Well, not exactly; maybe I'll make my fee one of your small paintings."

Leslie's warm vindicating smile helped to relieve my tension. I searched for the right words to express my gratitude.

"Leslie, if a painting is all you want, I can do better than that. I'd like to show my appreciation by painting your portrait, life size. But nothing I can give you will be worth what you are doing for my family and me."

"A Mark DeLouise portrait of me will be truly valued. I'll certainly do every-thing possible to prove your innocence." Leslie continued on with irrelevant chatter, but I was hearing her telepathic message ("It will not just be up to me. We are both in this together. The 'force' has called on us for some special task. Eventually, we will learn what this is all about.") And for other possible ears as well as mine, she assured me that, "I am working to get you back to your studio so I can collect."

When it was time for her to leave, she promised to keep in touch. "Just hold on. We're going to win."

Back in my cell, I thought again about how lucky I was to know Leslie. My hope in getting through this nightmare was boosted by knowing that the "force" had really developed a relationship with her.

Gracie would be grateful when she learned that Leslie had offered to accept a painting as payment. For me, the work would be a creative challenge. I looked forward to painting her Asian grace. Leslie was in her late thirties; five feet six, slender and shapely. Her shiny black hair was bobbed just below her ears. Whether for business or pleasure, she always dressed well. I did not want to ignore her almond-eyed Asian beauty, but, with abstract expression, I would need to go beyond this to image her full dimensions. I would need to make people see her soul, the soul that not only made her our good friend, but enabled her to develop a relationship with the "force."

As my vision of Leslie faded, anxieties relating to the trial surfaced in my mind. How might a jury react to my UFO story? I imagined that the prosecutor would rip such a defense apart, attacking me for what he would see as a stupid ruse.

Soon the media would respond. Their predators would sniff the air for the incriminating stench of guilt or the exonerating aroma of the innocent. Either way, it would be a sensational story. Eventually Hollywood might even take an interest, as film-makers and producers saw another way to make money.

I wondered how many of my fellow artists would stand by me. How many, on the other hand, would believe the accusation and see me as a pariah? I hated to think that some who I had considered friends might be unwilling to support me. While I imagined these wheels of probability spinning, I clung to my faith in God. I knew that Gracie and Sarah kept me in their prayers, and wondered if they would be going to church on Sunday. How might they explain my absence from the service?

As long as the FBI wanted to keep its investigation secret, they would release no reports of my arrest. They hoped they could build a case against me. They believed that they could break me down; so that I would reveal some plot against America that they presumed I was part of. Who on the "inside" could possibly have photographed the details of *Number 10* and sent the picture to me? There was no evidence on our computer, or anywhere else. They could not find evidence that was not there. I feared, however, that they could fabricate it. But they would still be utterly frustrated in their efforts to find the links they believed crucial to finding my "contacts". Trapped in the darkness of a limited reality, they could not see the futility of their investigation. Doggedly, they would push on.

In the meantime, they would need "damage control" for the already exposed image of *Number 10*. Strangely, they had allowed the painting to remain on public view until the last day of the exhibition. It was "out of the barn," so to speak. Many photographs of it had been taken and a few even published. But if they could never reveal what this painting actually represented, how could they find me guilty? Perhaps they would claim that the image was wrong, but that it proved my subversive intent. Pressure would be put on those who had the picture to turn it in to federal agents and "forget" it.

Chapter 13

HOME

Finally the day came. When I heard the sound of the guard's key unlocking my cell, I knew that it meant my freedom, at least for now. I was not supposed to know, but I did.

"Your lawyer's here, DeLouise."

It was McKenzie. This time his grudging tone was music to my ears. Soon I recognized the sound of Leslie's footsteps approaching the outer gate. My heart beat excitedly. McKenzie led me down the corridor to where she stood, waiting to greet me with a big, bright smile.

"Hey, they tell me you're going home today, Mark!"

I feigned surprise: "What?!"

"That's right, my friend. We just need to sign the release forms and we're out of here."

As we walked toward the administration office, I kept up the pretense.

"Leslie, what legal magic did you use to get me released without bail? What is going on?"

Leslie was in no mood to play.

"Let's just sign these papers and get out of here. You need to get home to your wife and daughter."

After signing my release, we went to the property office to recover my personal belongings. Then we walked to the exit, where we were met and escorted by a cordon of police officers. Outside were crowds of people, some supportive, some hostile. There were reporters and TV camera crews and curious passers-by.

We were guided to a car, beside which Agents Burns and Symes were standing. As Symes went around to the driver's side, Burns politely ushered us into the rear seats. From behind the dark glass of the limousine windows, we watched the police, attempting to disperse the crowd. A scuffle, apparently ignited by racist chants, was quickly brought under control. Two reporters had managed to get through the police line to within a few feet of our car, but we were already pulling away from the curb, into the afternoon traffic.

Leslie and I settled back into our seats with relief. No words were necessary. Our only talk related to my gratitude at going home.

At Christopher Street, six blocks south of Westbeth, we were met by two squad cars and escorted to the building's West Street entrance, where a crowd, much like the one we had escaped downtown, had attempted to gather. Blue barriers had been set up to keep traffic out of the area and people away. Police and news helicopters hovered overhead. Two of the officers accompanied us into the building and up the less-trafficked elevator to our floor, where another officer, a young Black woman, stood guard at our apartment door. I was relieved to have seen very few of our Westbeth neighbors. I hoped that their absence came from sensitive respect.

I could have used my key to enter, but, having Leslie with me, I rang the bell to alert Gracie and Sarah of our arrival. Exhilaration surged through me.

"Daddy!" Sarah and Gracie had to know it was me before they even opened the door. I entered, into their waiting arms. We held each other tight in the oneness of our relief. Then we each extended our embrace to Leslie, in gratitude for her friendship and counsel.

From the kitchen below I smelled the aroma of eggplant cooked in olive oil and Italian herbs. Gracie had prepared one of my favorite meals, eggplant parmesan, so welcome after weeks of prison food.

Sharing dinner together seemed blissful, even though we were mindful that our conversation was bugged. Guarding our words, we shared accounts of our experiences while separated and our joy that we could now resume our lives as family and members of community. Leslie crafted her comments and suggestions to reinforce our confidence.

We were all curious to see the TV reports of my release. We watched and listened intently as the crowd scene outside the Metropolitan Correctional Center appeared on the screen. Excitement grew when Leslie and I appeared, flanked by police. On television, the scene seemed even wilder than our experience. The supportive chanting, racist ranting, and honking, beeping, gridlocked traffic seemed like a Hollywood production. Significantly, there was a report from an unidentified source that the FBI could not keep DeLouise in custody because they lacked evidence. The case, however, was still under world-wide investigation.

As the report ended, and I was moving to turn off the television, the phone rang.

"It's for you, Dad," said Sarah. "It's Larry King from CNN."

Although I had been trying to avoid the media, I chose, not without some anxiety, to speak to King. As major an audience as his, I could at least hear what King had to say.

"Congratulations on your release, Mr. DeLouise. I'm calling to invite you to join me on my show. The public needs to hear from you. Will that be possible, sir?"

Perhaps the public did need to hear from me. But with the world wide investigation of my case continuing, I knew I had to be cautious. I would have to consult with Leslie. I told Larry King that I would consider it.

As soon as I hung up the phone, Leslie responded.

"You handled that well, Mark. I don't know who else may have gotten your phone number, but there is a good chance that it's not just CNN. More television people will be trying to reach you as well as reporters for newspapers and magazines, book publishers and even movie-makers. I'll wager that producers and screenwriters are already conferring as we speak, wondering how your story will turn out and how best it can be adapted to the screen."

Sarah giggled nervously, excited by the prospect of such attention, but understanding that it could not come without harassment. Gracie began to tense. Once a very private family, we were now notoriously public. Leslie continued,

"Now is not the time for interviews. Wait until you have been completely vindicated. Then your spotlight will be for celebration. Persons in the media may or may not believe in your innocence, but either way, it is better for you to keep a low profile.

"Right now, among all your contacts, be very discerning as to whom you can trust. Even your families need to be checked out. And, although it won't be easy, try for some normalcy. If you feel at some point that you just need to get away, let me know. I can help."

Assuming that our home was bugged, I did not ask Leslie how she could help. Perhaps, I hoped, she might be offering her country place.

Leslie's counsel and support were overwhelming. There were tears in Gracie's eyes. Even Sarah looked teary-eyed, but I was not ready to show emotion.

Regaining her composure, Gracie offered us all a simple dessert of brandied fruit. Leslie expressed her pleasure with this choice, and with the entire meal.

"It has been so good to be together again. Your hospitality has been wonderful, but I must get home. I have work to finish before bed. You know I'll be staying with you on this."

As she said "good-night," we all embraced. Outside the door there was a new police guard, a young Latino. Gracie had told me that the posting of the guards had begun the day before, and that squad cars were stationed at entry points around the building. Because I was the presumed link to their imagined spy ring, they had to keep me safe and closely watched.

Now that Leslie had left, she telepathically confirmed that she was indeed offering her country place. Beyond her loyalty as a friend, she understood that we were all involved in a galactic responsibility.

It was not yet 10 o'clock. There was still time to make a few contacts: our parents, of course, and our neighbors Sam and Josie, who had been so helpful to Gracie and Sarah while I was in prison. They had led support for me and them within the Wesbeth community. After we sent Sarah off to bed, we could at last share the intimacy for which we had longed.

In the morning I called Dr. Jonas, chief of my service at Meredith General. While he and my co-workers had no doubts of my innocence, some of the patients had fallen right into the government's conspiracy theory, sharing, it seemed, in a less defended and more psychotic way, the pathology of the FBI. I would, therefore, need to be reassigned to a facility related to the hospital, but physically separate from it. Dr. Jonas felt that my skills would be useful there, but that even with this select group of patients, I should only be known as "Mark." I could not use an alias, but they did not need to know my last name. Arrangements were being made for me to start this assignment next week.

The door guards left in about ten days. The FBI had monitored the public mood and decided that I was no longer at risk. The squad cars outside our building exits were now less obvious, and we were able to walk outdoors without getting more than a few double-takes. At school, most of Sarah's peers seemed less concerned about who her father was. My new work assignment was working out, and Gracie continued her teaching responsibilities with fewer awkward questions. Most in our church had welcomed us, and many held us in their prayers. In short, we were leading almost normal lives.

Of course, our experience with the UFO, my production of *Number 10*, our development of telepathic powers, and our ongoing contacts with the little Orb, were anything but normal. Nor could our lives be "normal," as long as I was the object of an espionage investigation.

We knew that we were under constant FBI surveillance.

Although there was nothing for them to find, we feared that they might fabricate a link in order to frame me. And if they did, I would be back in prison again. The residue of doubt that lingered in the minds of some of those with whom we seemed to have, at least on the surface, positive relations, might then turn to disbelief in my innocence. It would be that way until the whole story, the true story, was told; but even I did not know the whole story.

Gracie knew most of what I knew, and Sarah knew what she needed to know, as did Leslie. There were certain things that the little Orb had instructed me not to reveal to anyone. I didn't like keeping things from Gracie, but I thought it best to cooperate fully with the "force."

Gracie had added caller ID to our telephone account right after my arrest. She had also intended to get an unlisted number, but strangely the few hostile calls had ceased and there had been no intrusive calls since the one from Barry King. Nor had there been any hostile mail, other than official communications relating to my case. As Gracie and I discussed the fact that our phone number was still listed, I sensed another presence in the room. It was the little Orb, who for the first time would be communicating with the two of us together. Our case-related calls and mail, the little Orb explained, and even our email, were being monitored by the "force." Anything dangerous or threatening, or even merely annoying was intercepted and terminated.

A few days later, as Gracie and I were relaxing in the living room, the phone rang. Gracie picked up; her greeting indicating that the call was from Leslie. As cordialities continued, I heard Gracie respond with, " …working hard pretending to be normal. Fortunately there are some good supportive people out here."

"Eventually I heard, "I'll call you back after I discuss this with Mark. This week-end might work."

Week-end. Could this be our awaited invitation to the country? If it was, why did Leslie use the telephone that she knew was being tapped? Perhaps she assumed that there would be no way to keep it secret anyway with the constant surveillance of our comings and goings. I waited for Gracie to fill me in on Leslie's side of the conversation.

"Leslie wants to know if we are ready for a break. She's inviting us to her country place for the week-end, or longer if we choose."

It sounded like good timing for all of us. Leslie had mentioned earlier that her fiancé, a surgeon, would be away for a conference. His name was Steve. He and Leslie frequently spent play/work time together at her cabin, but this week-end he would be presenting a paper at the School of Medicine at the University of Chicago. Although to some extent, Steve also was our friend, we would be more comfortable with him away. He knew quite a bit about our case and would have been "cool," but, if we needed to communicate telepathically, he would be out of the loop. We needed to have Leslie to ourselves.

We were beginning to feel that, for now, our routines were under control, but not without stress. Some time away might help.

"Call her right back," I said. "We're ready."

The plan was set. Since I was on a new work schedule, I could be home by early Friday afternoon. Leslie would pick me and our gear up at Westbeth, then Sarah from school, and lastly Gracie from the school where she taught. We would try to get on the road before traffic leaving the city got too heavy.

At 2:30 on Friday, Leslie was waiting for me on Bethune Street. As I got into her car, she telepathically called my attention to a car parked down the block and across the street, predicting,

"As soon as we leave, that car will pull out and follow us."

We both assumed that she had spotted the fed's surveillance car. Might this have been avoided if our planning for the trip had been telepathic? It did not seem likely, as they monitored all my comings and goings from the building.

The car did follow us. And when we stopped at Public School 41 for Sarah, it also stopped, several cars behind, waiting for us to move on. At Gracie's school, it followed the same routine, but when we got into the mix and merge of highway traffic, we lost sight of it. Based on what we had seen in the movies, we assumed their tracking information was being relayed from vehicle to vehicle. Make, model, color, plate number, and expected route would be passed from agent to agent. Already they knew certain details of our plans, but they wanted on-the-spot surveillance. We expected that Leslie's cabin would be bugged.

Even knowing that we continued to be observed, getting away was a relief. We spent a lot of time outdoors, blessed by the sun in unusually warm early October. Arboreal beauty, fresh flora scented breezes, the sounds of birds by day and crickets after dark put us in touch with the possibility of an uncorrupted world. Sarah discovered a brook nearby and a local boy with a puppy. They played together while we adults lazed about.

Leslie shared her culinary tradition by fixing food unlike anything we had ever known from Chinese restaurants. She continued to see to our comfort, refusing our offer to help, until Gracie convinced her that she must eat my "ultimate" banana pancakes. So on Sunday, the kitchen was mine for making brunch. Then we all made new discoveries in the woods, as we helped collect dry twigs for the fireplace.

Then, while Gracie and Sarah helped Leslie prepare supper, I used the late day sun and shadows to finish a nature sketch. After dinner we played charades and shared jokes, stories and poetry, until our yawns and heavy eyelids brought our day to a close.

As I lay in bed next to Gracie, I could not help but think about the unreality of this retreat. Leaving our stressful world behind, we did not even have to pretend that we were any different than normal week-enders.

Monday morning we loaded into Leslie's car for the trip home. I drove, so that Leslie could review notes for her afternoon meeting. Down the road I saw a black van, and when it started up, it seemed that once again we were being followed. We had not let our awareness of the FBI's ongoing surveillance spoil our week-end. We would just ignore the van. Whatever the FBI saw or heard, it would not be what they were hoping for.

When we arrived in our block, we said grateful good-byes, and

Leslie drove off. We gathered up our belongings, as friendly neighbors acknowledged our return, offering a buffer to harsh reality. While many of our neighbors were indifferent and a few even hostile, I was glad that the friendly ones were in the majority. We would learn if that would remain true with time. As we approached our apartment door, we heard our phone ringing. Before I could get my keys, the ringing stopped, but we heard the machine message as we entered. It was our pastor, Jim Daniels. I would return his call after I used the bathroom.

Sarah had already beaten me to the bathroom. Hearing my "Oh, no," she assured me that she would be right out. Gracie was behind me. As I got my turn, I could not help but reflect on this painful, yet welcome, competition. This was something I missed in prison.

When I got downstairs, I played back Jim's message. He had been away because his father died, but was now eager to meet with us. He had been in North Carolina dealing with family business, helping his mother and other family members and had just returned in time for yesterday's worship service. He had expected to see us in church, but of course we were not there. My arrest had been a focus of the congregation.

I returned his call, extending condolences. Jim thanked me, but said that his real concern was me. While a student intern had stood in for him, he had felt uncomfortable about not being around at the time of my release.

"We did miss you," I admitted, "but really felt sorry for your loss. We weren't in church yesterday because we had an invitation to the country. We spent the week-end in Woodstock with Leslie Chen – not only our lawyer, but our good friend. We should have told people we would be away."

"I'm sure that you really needed to get away. You don't have to be in church to worship, but we did miss you. You know how it is with us pastors. We are so preoccupied with keeping members of our flock together where we can see and count them that we cannot imagine that they might need other nurture. God has blessed you with a friend like Leslie. I remember meeting her some time ago."

No need to apologize. You have really been in our corner – the support you gave to Gracie and Sarah while I was in prison, the clear thinking you shared with the congregation on my behalf, your prayers. I am so grateful.

"Thanks, Mark. I could not do it alone. God really does strengthen us, and we in the church strengthen each other."

"Gracie and I will work something out to see you soon. And we will be in church next Sunday."

At church next Sunday, we were, for the most part, warmly greeted. Some of the members, however, seemed to relate awkwardly. Jim seemed unusually ebullient, perhaps as a defense against anxiety relating to some of the congregational response.

Although we had received some support from the church, it was not surprising that many in the community had questions, some of which we feared were hostile. Jim had to be aware of this. He aimed his sermon at mature discernment, love, and loyalty to Christ. His text was Ephesians 4: 14-16.

We must no longer be children, tossed to and fro and blown about by every wind of doctrine, by people's trickery, by their craftiness in deceitful scheming. But speaking truth in love, we must grow up in every way into Him who is the head, into Christ, from whom the whole body, joined and knit together by every ligament with which it is equipped, as each part is working properly, promotes the body's growth in building itself up in love.

Jim admitted that my *Number 10* was a puzzle, but pointed out how illogical the charges against me were. He questioned the "deceitful scheming" of those who had imprisoned me and were continuing to monitor my life, and called on everyone to "grow up in every way." Loyalty was owed to God's community, which was not the state. He called for all to speak "the truth in love."

After the service, some of the doubtful seemed more open to reason. Besieged with questions, the three of us stayed together, supporting each other in our responses. We understood the value in this process, but still felt a need to escape. Sensing our discomfort, Jim spread his arms wing-like around us, signaling to the congregation our need for privacy. He assured us that he would be in touch.

Chapter 14

FOREIGN INTRIGUE

When we returned home, there was a message from Leslie on our answering machine. I called at once.

"Mark, did you hear the news?"

We had heard no news since yesterday. I assumed it was a reference to my case.

"You are not alone, my friend. Today's news is that a Russian artist, Vladimir Ivanov, has been charged with espionage. Are you sitting down, Mark? ... Ivanov is said to have exhibited a painting depicting a top-secret military installation, which even most of the high ranking Russian government officials knew nothing of."

"My God!"

"It's getting deeper and deeper. Check it out for yourselves. I'm not going to stay on the phone now. I just want you to turn on CNN and we'll talk later."

Gracie had been waiting to hear why Leslie had called. "It's on the news," I said. "Call Sarah and we'll all find out."

I turned on the TV, which was recycling commercials, as we all assembled to see what Leslie had called about. "I'm not alone," I explained briefly. "There is another artist like me. Just wait for the story to come on."

It did not take long for this top story to return. CNN's Moscow correspondent, Kirsten Slater, was attempting to interview one of the Russian bureaucrats, but getting very little information. There was then an interview with a friend of the Russian artist, who said that the charges against Ivanov could not be true. He not only could not believe them, but said that he did not believe "the American" guilty either. Still another report presented street interviews from New York and Atlanta, which echoed the obvious connection.

There was no official reaction yet from Washington, but we pondered what the feds might be thinking. Previously, some had suggested that, as emerging capitalists, Russia's competitive needs might lead to espionage against the United States. Now, however, with security violated in both countries, the nations would suspect a common enemy; perhaps an international counter-cultural conspiracy.

Later that evening, while puttering around in my studio, a familiar feeling told me that I had a visitor. The little Orb had come with an unsettling message: I was to be subpoenaed to appear before a grand jury. It assured me, however, that the "force" would be there to assist me in my responses as needed. There would be a week's time for my family and me to prepare ourselves for whatever came after the hearing.

"Use your telepathic skills to share this information with your family and your lawyer," I was instructed, "but call your lawyer openly when you receive the subpoena."

The subpoena came on Wednesday morning. As I was about to enter my car for my drive to work, a man approached with it. He had known what time I would leave and which car was mine. Another man was observing us from their car across the street. The little Orb's forewarning and assurance helped me to keep my anger hidden.

On my drive to work, I thought about the questioning I would have to face. Later, in grand rounds, I had to make a special effort to focus on my responsibility for patient reports, and listen to the clinical observations of my colleagues. My personal battle with confidence and doubt was a distraction.

After lunch I called Leslie to report that I had received the subpoena. Because of our earlier telepathic communication, she already expected this, but feigned surprise for the benefit of surveillance.

"I can meet with you Saturday, three to five, my place, and again on Sunday, as long as we're finished by eight.

"I'll be at your place Saturday. On Sunday, why don't you come here for lunch? Maybe two o'clock?"

Assuming that this would not be a problem for Gracie, it was settled. There would be certain details covered openly in these meetings, but other aspects of my preparation would be telepathically communicated.

That evening, I received instructions from the "force." I was to draw in detail the bathroom adjoining the master bedroom of the prosecuting attorney conducting the hearing. It was to include the exact placement of items in the medicine cabinet, design of towels, etc. I would take the drawing to the hearing in a 9" by 12" envelope and present it to the prosecutor, as my cued response to a question the little Orb knew she would ask. Telepathically, I shared this plan with Gracie and Leslie.

I took our pen and paper. The "force" again directed my work; this time only a drawing, but with information sure to baffle my inquisitor. As I reflected on the potential of this project, I wondered what was happening to my counterpart, Vladimir Ivanov. I wondered what he might be thinking, how the Russian authorities were dealing with him, and most of all, what was his contact with the "force." Then, as sometimes it chose to do, the little Orb appeared, responding to my thoughts. It told me that Vladimir and I would be able to communicate telepathically. We could share experience and support each other. This prospect brought me a surge of excitement. As stressed as I was, I had to feel privilege.

The little Orb told me that I could not tell even Gracie or Leslie of this new contact until Vladimir and I were both vindicated. It reported that Vladimir was in solitary confinement in a maximum security prison. Each night he meditated before going to sleep. This would be around two p.m. New York time, the optimum time to make connection.

During the next few days, I was under pressure to tie up loose ends before I might once again be imprisoned, leaving Gracie and Sarah on their own. At work, my clinical reports had to be up to date. My anxiety level was high, but anticipation of conversations with Vladimir provided compensation.

I arranged my schedule so that I could try to contact Vladimir at the appropriate time. On Friday, taking a late lunch break, I opened a bag lunch in the privacy of my office, and reflected on scripture I had read the night before. Could the Book of Revelation set the tone for making my telepathic connection? I read about Satan's doom. Literally it made no sense. The liberal church avoided it, but my background in apocalyptic writing helped me understand the symbolism. Perhaps my extra-terrestrial contacts had led me to this text.

When the thousand years are ended, Satan will be released from his prison and will come out to deceive the nations at the four corners of the earth, Gog and Magog, in order to gather them for battle ... (Rev 20: 7)

Evil spirits were ruling the nations, and Vladimir and I were both victims of the nations that they ruled. Satan's defeat was promised, but for now, the struggle continued.

Suddenly I was startled by the sound of a distant voice from above, calling my name. I waited for it to be repeated. Almost five minutes went by. Had someone called me? Could it be Vladimir, as I had hoped? Was he waiting for my response?

"Comrade!" I ventured. Is that you, Vladimir?"

"It is I," the voice responded.

I could not imagine that Vladimir would be speaking English, but perhaps translation was part of the telepathic process. Briefly we shared our experiences. He said that he was hearing me in Russian, so translation was indeed part of the arrangement.

Like me, Vladimir had focused much of his creative work on protests against unjust structures, and solidarity with working class resistance. In spite of the failures of the Soviet Union, Vladimir had created art which celebrated its successes and expressed hope in a real worker's state. His work had protested counter-revolution and attempted to inspire real communism. I learned that he was two years younger than I; his wife was Galima and his children were Nikolai, age 7, and Alexandra, age nine (the same age as Sarah).

Vladimir's imprisonment was harsh. There were many interrogation sessions aimed at breaking him down and making him "confess" and name other "spies." He longed to be at home with his family, as I was.

"I am thankful to be home now," I said, "but I may yet be returned to prison. I am under constant surveillance. We must be strong. I believe that our co-operation with the "force" may be critical – for our world and theirs."

To some extent, my faith was inspired by my reflection on scripture. I felt privileged to be able to connect to the ancient texts. I assumed that Vladimir was unfamiliar with the text, but wondered if, were he to read it, he might not understand it better than most who considered themselves "Christian." I recalled that Karl Marx's friend, Frederick Engels, who didn't have the advantage of modern Biblical scholarship, was able to grasp the essence of the Book of Revelation, even though much of his historical reference for it was incomplete and even wrong.

"I, too, believe we are serving a good purpose," Vladimir responded. "I believe we will be vindicated."

As "Christian" and "atheist," we shared a bond of "faith." It was, in fact, a "faith" based in experience, pointing to something beyond ourselves, whether found in ancient texts or life struggles. It was something that might or might not be called "God."

We had now lost contact. The little Orb appeared, congratulating me on my successful communication and explaining that the communication had ended because a guard had come by Vladimir's cell. Even though it was "after hours," there were sometimes prisoner checks. In those few moments of contact, however, we had established a foundation for kinship. Wondering if our families also would connect, I imagined how exciting it would be for Sarah to communicate with Vladimir's children. Reading my thoughts, the little Orb assured me that when our innocence was clear, all in our families would spend time together. Then my guide left. It was time for me to get back to work.

Over the week-end, as planned, I met with Leslie; privately on Saturday and then with Gracie and Sarah on Sunday, to help them understand what might or might not happen. My immediate future looked bad, but I was confident of the long run.

Chapter 15

THE HEARING

The day of the grand jury hearing had arrived. With the 9" x 12" envelope containing my drawing of the prosecutor's bathroom, I headed for Bethune Street to meet Leslie. If there was any respect for logic, my drawing which the little Orb had directed, would prove my innocence. If no "spy" created the bathroom drawing, no "spy" had created *Number 10*.

But I could not expect logical thinking. Both my painting and the drawing would provoke serious questions. My family and I hoped for the best, but were prepared for my return to prison.

On my way to Leslie's car, I was stopped by a man who identified himself as an FBI agent.

"Mr. DeLouise, I'm Agent Kelly, Federal Bureau of Investigation. How 'ya doing, sir?"

"Fine, thanks. What's this about?"

"Agent Walker and I are taking you and your attorney down to the courthouse. Ms. Chen might not get you there on time in this heavy rush. And more importantly, there's been a leak of information about the hearing. We expect a siege of both domestic and foreign press and a crowd of curious spectators.

"'A leak'? Should we believe that you were trying to keep the hearing secret, Agent Kelly?"

"Perhaps not. But this shouldn't be an issue. Right now, we need to move quickly.

"Ms. Chen, you double parked right beside our car. The space is legal; so if you just back up and let Agent Walker pull out, you can park there. Then you and Mr. DeLouise will ride with us. We'll bring you back here after the hearing."

It seemed that we were in protective custody. We turned up West Street; then across Twelfth and down Seventh Avenue. The car siren gave us the right-of-way. Leslie and I talked only of traffic and weather. When we had talked on the phone earlier, Leslie made it clear that she was committed to my case and confident that we had more to count on than her skill and my innocence.

"Knowing how this system works," she had said, "there may be more tough hurdles ahead. Eventually, though, we'll get through this. Your back-up won't fail you."

I remembered almost every word of our conversation. I hadn't worried about the surveillance, since the reference to "back-up" could easily have meant my religious faith. That would be consistent with the FBI profile of me.

As we neared the courthouse, we could see the expected crowds. The police moved to clear the courthouse steps of spectators. By forming a protective cordon, they made it possible for us to avoid reporters and cameras. Once inside, we were lead to the hearing room on the second floor. Before we entered, Agent Kelly explained the procedure, just as Leslie had. Although my lawyer could not be with me in the hearing room, she would be assigned to an adjoining area where she would be available for counsel.

Two guards equipped with side arms flanked the door. Once inside, I was greeted with stern scrutiny – from the judge, the prosecutor and several of the sixteen jurors. Other jurors were harder to read, while some seemed (not unexpectedly) curious. The stenographer's prim aloofness signaled that her only aim was to do her job efficiently. I was ushered to a small table equipped with a mike, where I sat down to face the jury.

As I waited, I became more than just visually aware of the

discussion between the prosecutor and the judge. The little Orb, seen only by me, had amplified their words for my ears and, as I was told, for Leslie's in the other room. Leslie had been enabled to hear everything from the grand jury room, and, of course, we maintained telepathic access.

Daniel Burns, Timothy Bennett and Colonel William F. Carrington arrived together. They were seated at a table about ten feet to my right, each with a mike. I noted the Bible on their table and reflected on its function in the court – for them and for myself. Why was this sacred text used to facilitate human law? How could it demand honest testimony in a profane court? Until advised otherwise, I certainly would avoid truth relating to my extra-terrestrial contacts.

Minutes passed, punctuated by the sounds of intermittent coughing among the jurors and the riffling of papers by the prosecutor, judge, and three main witnesses, as they checked over their briefs. The judge, Michael J. Simpson, looked up sternly from his bench, again staring for a moment. I wondered how this African-American man would look at me. I recalled the complicity of the Jewish judge in the notoriously unjust condemnation and cruel execution of the Rosenbergs. But whatever Simpson's orientation, how much power did he actually have? What might have already been decided at higher levels? Was it not in their interest to appoint an African American to make it all appear "fair"?

Of course, I was not yet a defendant. The results of the hearing had yet to be determined, but I had no reason to trust the process. The hearing began with Simpson's nod to the prosecuting attorney, Leona Fischer, who came forward to the center of the room, faced the grand jury and said,

"Ladies and gentlemen, we have a task of great importance. You were chosen to accomplish this task justly and efficiently. You will hear the testimonies of three government witnesses and the accused; after which you will be asked to indict the accused. He is accused of espionage against the United States, in the service of a foreign nation, the identity of which is yet unknown to us. The government must prove the accused culpable, based on the sworn testimony and evidence presented here by the witnesses. The accused has been called for the exercise of his right to give rebuttal testimony, to which you will give your strict attention and impartial consideration. You are not here to determine the guilt or innocence of the accused, but to decide whether or not he should be required to appear before a trial jury for that purpose. Judge Michael J. Simpson will be presiding over this hearing to see that grand jury procedure is strictly adhered to."

She then turned to the judge, who nodded, signaling her to begin the next procedural stage.

"Your Honor, the people call Agent Daniel Burns of the Federal Bureau of Investigation to testify regarding the Mark DeLouise/ *Number10* case."

Fischer continued with the swearing in and routine instructions, which Burns followed. She then proceeded with questions aimed at my incrimination.

"Agent Burns, when, and under what circumstances did you first meet Mr. Mark DeLouise?"

"I first met Mr. DeLouise in mid-September of this year at an art exhibit opening at the Westbeth Gallery, located in the same building where DeLouise resides, in the West Village area of Manhattan."

"And what transpired there?"

"Well, while viewing the paintings in the section of the gallery where Mr. DeLouise's works were displayed, I was attracted to a painting entitled *Number 10*."

"What in particular attracted you to that painting?"

"The fact that it was so much unlike any of his other paintings displayed there."

"It was that different?"

Prompted by Fischer, Burns went on to describe the painting. "It contained what appeared to be the inside of a building which not only drew my interest, but my serious concern. I felt the need to get a closer look, to make sure that I was really seeing what I thought I saw."

"And what was that?"

"My inspection of the meticulously drawn details convinced me that I was seeing objects of military significance."

"Were you able to identify the building?"

"No. I knew I had to seek information from a knowledgeable source to understand what I was seeing. I began by taking pictures of the painting, one with Mr. DeLouise standing next to it. I sent the pictures to the agency director, who brought them to the attention of experts in the Department of Defense, who gave them to the Chairman of the Joint Chiefs of Staff. I also brought my friend, Col. William F. Carrington, to Westbeth Gallery to see the painting."

Burns explained that he wanted Carrington to serve as another witness. Later, he showed him the photograph.

"And what was his reaction?"

"Wouldn't you rather let him tell you that, Counselor?"

"That's a good suggestion, Agent Burns. I will move on to my question about how Mr. DeLouise related to your reactions, and those of the Colonel. Did he appear concerned?"

"No, but he must have been. I'd say he was a good actor as well as a good painter."

"Agent Burns, you told us that you sent copies of the pictures you took of the *Number 10* painting to the FBI director, who brought them to the attention of experts from the Department of Defense, and to the Chairman of the Joint Chiefs of Staff, in order to determine whether or not the painting depicted something that really exists which might be of sensitive military significance."

"Yes."

"And what was the result?"

"The painting depicted the interior of a building that does exist. Its location, content and purpose are classified top-secret."

"So, is it the fact of this building's actual existence and its top-secret classification which led to Mr. DeLouise being suspected of espionage?"

"Yes, precisely."

"And what did you learn from your further investigation of Mr. DeLouise?"

"That he is a very clever operative who knows he's being closely watched and has so far succeeded in covering his tracks."

While Dan Burns fielded the prosecutor's questions, I watched the faces of the jurors and the judge for expressions that might give me clues to what they were thinking. They, in turn, seemed to be looking for my reaction. Some looked angry, perhaps determined to condemn, while others looked puzzled. Judge Simpson succeeded in avoiding discernable expression. Each time I glanced in his direction, he would quickly shift his gaze away, toward the direction of the prosecuting attorney and the witnesses.

Leona Fischer then questioned Col. Carrington and Agent Bennett. I was next. But before that could begin, Fischer asked to approach the bench. As she and the judge conferred, I observed the jury – shifting in their seats and here and there a nervous cough or a throat clearing. The witnesses were whispering to each other. Then Fischer turned and walked toward me, as if stalking prey.

"Your Honor, the people call Mr. Mark DeLouise to testify regarding the Mark DeLouise/*Number 10* Case."

I sensed in Fischer, aggressive political ambition. Her attractive 5'10" figure seemed a tower of determination to bring me down. But her threatening image was countered by my knowledge that I would be ready for her with a perplexing surprise – my detailed drawing of her intimate space. I hoped that my opportunity to show the drawing would come soon.

She began with a few basic questions relating to my employment and creative work. She wanted the court to know what kinds of things I usually painted.

"My work often comments on economic, cultural and political injustice and the pathology of war."

"So, are you what is called a social-realist painter?"

"You might say that."

"And what do you say, Mr. DeLouise? Please answer 'yes' or 'no'."

"Yes."

"Where do you usually exhibit your work?"

"Galleries, museums, churches and universities."

"Nationally and internationally?"

"Yes."

"Where internationally?"

"France, the USSR, Germany, Nigeria, Viet Nam."

"You exhibited your paintings in the USSR and Viet Nam. Did you visit these countries while your work was exhibited there, or at any other time?"

"No."

Fischer already had that information. The FBI had thoroughly checked me out, but Fischer wanted the jury to hear about my exhibitions in questionable places. Even though the USSR was no more, and both Russia and Viet Nam were now victims of global capital, history suggested that I might be sympathetic to communism. This might increase suspicion against me. I hoped that some in the jury would have positive recall of Glasnost, and some an understanding of the shared anguish of the Viet Nam War. Odds, however, were against me. I felt a desperate need for Leslie or the little Orb.

Of course, I had my drawing of the prosecutor's bathroom. This, it would seem, would prove that I did not need a subversive co-conspirator to produce a drawing of an off-limits place. If my drawing of Fischer's bathroom proved the illogic of their accusation, I could handle this by myself. But would the court be able to make the paradigm shift required to reach the sensible conclusion?

I waited for Fischer to ask the question that would give me the opportunity to test the court. Finally she asked,

"Mr. DeLouise, we know that you had to have an accomplice provide you with details for your *Number 10* painting. Do you really expect us to believe that you could show this top-secret military installation without the assistance of an inside traitor?"

"Whether you believe me or not, I have something here which I hope will convince everyone here that I am telling the truth."

I held up my envelope. She looked at it and at me; then turned to Judge Simpson, who nodded his approval that she take and open it. All looked on as she withdrew the mysterious contents from the envelope. When she lifted the cover sheet protecting the drawing, she seemed transfixed. Judge Simpson cleared his throat. Fischer's face was flushed with anger. She walked toward me and asked through clenched teeth,

"Where the hell did you get this?"

"Since it must be obvious to you what it is, shouldn't you be asking me how I got it rather than where?"

"All right then, Mr. DeLouise; how did you get this?"

"The same way I got the particulars that made the painting of *Number 10*."

She turned to Judge Simpson with the drawing. When she explained what it was, his own puzzled expression and glower in my direction made it clear that he would be of no help. The jurors and the three witnesses exchanged questioning glances.

Meanwhile, the little Orb made contact for a brief telepathic conference with Leslie and me to inform us of what to expect. Both the prosecutor and the judge, the little Orb said, were greatly threatened by my ability to produce such accuracy of details from Fischer's very personal area. Rather than prove my innocence, the mystery would lead to my indictment and I would be taken into custody to await trial.

The drawing that Leslie and I had thought would exonerate me would only increase suspicion! It was somewhat frightening to know that apparently no one on this jury would be able to think outside their conditioned context. Most in my own counter-cultural community would have seen the logic, but not this court. Why had the extra-terrestrials arranged for me to make this drawing if it would not prove my innocence? Perhaps the drawing would bring the members of the jury personal insight later on, after my vindication. Perhaps also, as an artist, I needed to appreciate the difficulty of reaching people's consciousness.

For now, the little Orb told us not to worry. Everything was proceeding according to plan. Still, I dreaded being locked away from my family again for God knows how long, waiting to be tried for a crime I didn't commit. I thought of Gracie and Sarah having to suffer the pain of our separation again. Yet, we all knew that we had to go along with the program. We had come this far. We would keep the faith, and I would keep my promise to stay the course until its purpose (which I believed to be a good one) was fully realized.

My reflection on our telepathic conference ended as I noted that the prosecutor and the judge had finished their consultation. I prepared to listen to what Fischer would say as she walked slowly toward the jury with the drawing in hand.

"Ladies and gentlemen, due to the very personal nature of the material presented to me by Mr. DeLouise, I am embarrassed to show this to you. I will, however, explain it in terms of its relationship to the *Number 10* painting which you also have not seen, and for security reasons will not see."

Fischer briefly described the relationship of the drawing to the painting, and then called Agent Burns to the stand.

"Agent Burns, is it true that from the time you ascertained that the *Number 10* painting done by Mr. DeLouise depicted in exact external and internal detail a top-secret U.S. military installation; he has been kept under strict investigative surveillance?"

"Yes, it is."

"Well, Agent Burns, I reside on the upper east side of Manhattan, in an area bordered on the north by 89th Street; on the south by 65th Street; on the west by Fifth Avenue; and on the east by First Avenue. During your strict surveillance of Mr. DeLouise, did he ever go anywhere within the area I just described?"

Burns related my few incursions into that area, none of which involved entering any apartment building.

Fischer was silent for a moment. Then she looked at the drawing again, and at me. Speaking from where she was, as if afraid to risk a closer encounter with the mystery man she saw me as, she said,

"Mr. DeLouise, if with this drawing your objective is to convince us that you are some kind of sorcerer, you may have succeeded. After hearing Agent Burns's testimony, I can think of no other explanation. How you managed to get the information which enabled you to do a painting depicting the exact details of a U.S. military installation is, I am sure, a matter in which the FBI is leaving no practical or theoretical possibility unexplored. The critical question we have both asked is: did you receive help from someone on the inside? You have denied this. Beyond denial, you have presented a very accurate drawing of objects as they are located and arranged in a private area of my home – presumably in an effort to convince us that you are telling the truth.

"Perhaps we should believe you. It seems quite impossible for anyone in my household to have made it possible for you to do this drawing. Furthermore, how would you have known that I would be prosecuting your case, and how would you have known where I live? And even knowing this, how could you have gotten through our very tight security system? In view of this, I ask you again, Mr. DeLouise (and remember you are still under oath) how did you obtain the information that enabled you to do *Number 10* and the drawing that you presented to me today?"

My cue came from the little Orb.

"Through a source that comes from far beyond this world."

Everyone stared in my direction. For some, the answer seemed so absurd that it could only be interpreted as an affront to the court. Others waited for some rational explanation, something that might contradict what they had heard. Some looked astonished, including even the normally restrained court stenographer. From Fischer came an expected response.

"Would you please repeat that, Mr. DeLouise?"

"Yes. I said, 'through a source that comes from far beyond this world'."

Glances were exchanged among the jurors. Others failed to suppress their murmurs. All waited for Fischer's response.

"This world? Do you mean this planet?"

"Yes, this planet."

Fischer had just expressed her confidence that the FBI would leave no explanation unexplored. The intervention of extra-terrestrials, however, was beyond her imagination and presumably beyond the imagination of the FBI as well. I wondered if her look of contempt was a mask, covering feelings of confusion or even despair. Within, however, a legalistic context, communication from outer space was a difficult leap. She could not allow herself to think that I might be telling the truth. She looked at the judge, then the jury – hoping for validation. Then her fleeting smile suggested that she saw what she needed. She was ready to make her summation.

"Ladies and gentlemen," she began. "You have heard the testimonies of the three key witnesses in this case and the testimony of the accused, Mr. Mark DeLouise. Consider very carefully all that you have heard and especially what Mr. DeLouise has explained to the court regarding how he did the *Number 10* painting and the drawing presented to me here. His explanation is that he was enabled (and here I quote), 'Through a source that comes from far beyond this world.' And when I asked him to clarify this, he stated most emphatically that he did indeed mean from far beyond this planet. In these times of so-called extra-terrestrial sightings, and movies with 'alien' themes, some may be inclined to believe such a claim. Believable or not, in one way or another, Mr. DeLouise has apparently been able to break through the barriers of forbidden territories – a top-secret U.S. military installation and my very own well-secured private residence. This makes him an extremely dangerous man; a threat to our national and personal security. Although we have no evidence actually placing him at the two scenes of concern, I have no reasonable doubt that he has committed crimes of trespass, because of the concrete graphic evidence, which he has admitted producing under quite dubitable circumstances. Here, however, we are only concerned with whether or not he has committed a crime against the state, the crime of espionage. You now have the task of deciding if the evidence presented here substantiates criminal indictment. If you so find (and I hope you do), I will recommend that the accused be immediately remanded to custody, where he will await trial."

Since I had known what to expect, I was prepared to cover my anger with a cool façade. I recalled Leslie's instructions relating to my facial expressions and body language. As I would soon be actually on trial, I hoped that I had become an expert in defendant behavior skills.

While the grand jury deliberated, I was allowed to meet with Leslie for an evaluative discussion. Agents Kelly and Walker kept their eyes on us. Because the little Orb had made it possible for Leslie to have seen and heard the entire grand jury drama, she was better able to plan our next steps. Little more than two hours had gone by when Agent Kelly signaled that the deliberations were over. Telepathically, I would contact Gracie and Sarah to let them know what was happening.

As I entered the hearing room, Judge Simpson's eyes greeted me with what looked like compassion. But as he began the judicial litany that would spell out the next stage of the mystery drama in which I starred, his seemingly sympathetic expression changed to that of a man regretfully observing a pariah. It was as if, in a matter of seconds, I had gone from soul-brother to major threat. He could not take seriously my claim of extra-terrestrial contact and still maintain his role. If his first look was unguarded sympathy, it may have revealed belief in my testimony, which he must now strenuously deny.

Fisher's expression was arrogant satisfaction. As Simpson reviewed what had occurred and what was to come, I barely listened, since I had already been prepared. After the indictments came the arraignment. With Leslie now at my side, I entered "Not guilty" pleas to the charges of espionage and criminal trespass. The trial date set was in two months. With bail denied, I would continue to be away from my family. On the positive side, we had more time to prepare our defense, for which we could count on help from the little Orb.

Back in prison, some days went by slowly, others quickly, depending on what was happening inside and out. At first, crowds of friends and foes could be heard as before, shouting support or condemnation outside. Inside, I had to cope with hostility from most of the guards and some of the inmates. Even without the harassment, prison was a terrible place to be. Believing, however, that the force was in charge, I was equipped to tolerate my circumstance. Plus, I had the very special privilege of communicating telepathically with my family, Leslie, and the little Orb. In this manner, I was not only able to keep my family close, but hoped to receive information on my case from beyond.

Leslie described the expected court personae. Judge Simpson would be again presiding, and Leona Fischer would continue as prosecutor. A black middle-aged male and a young Korean female would be Fischer's assistants. Leslie would have two pro-bono associates, a white middle-aged male and a young Puerto Rican female. Each side chose a racial mix in an effort to appear fair. So far, we knew of only three government witnesses, so we hoped the trial would be short. The judge and the attorneys had reached a procedural agreement that the primary counselors would be the only ones questioning witnesses and the only presenters of opening and closing statements. Their colleagues would serve only an advisory capacity.

Chapter 16

＊ ———— ⚙ ———— ＊

THE TRIAL: DAY ONE

"**A**ll rise!"
With the usual order, the judge's entry was announced. He took his seat and told the people to be seated. He stated the title and the purpose of the case; introduced the prosecution and defense teams; explained the rules relating to court demeanor and called the attorneys to the bench. This was an opportunity for procedural questions and requests and remaining instructions.

It was the prosecution's privilege to begin the case. District Attorney Leona Fischer presented to everyone her opening statement, directed especially to the jury. The earlier stir subsided to almost silence.

"Ladies and Gentlemen, because of the very mysterious circumstances impinging on this case, this may prove to be the most challenging of my legal career. Yet, I accept it with great enthusiasm. I believe that the despicable crime of espionage has been committed against our country by one or more of its trusted citizens; that one of the perpetrators of that crime is present in this courtroom; and that with your intelligent and fair consideration of all the evidence presented, we, on behalf of the people of the United States, will bring this case against the defendant, Mark DeLouise, to its most just conclusion.

As Fischer spoke, her listeners were attentive, with only the normal, acceptable noise.

Then it was Leslie's turn. Stationed further from the jury, she had several more steps before reaching her spot. The earlier stir subsided to an almost silence. Only the slight sound of her own graceful movement could be heard until she began to speak.

"Ladies and Gentlemen, the case you will begin hearing today, especially you the members of the jury, for your careful consideration and just decision, is as the prosecution stated, a challenging one. And it is, the defense agrees, quite a mysterious one. Since this case came to the attention of the FBI, the President of the United States, the State Department, the Justice Department, the U.S. Congress, the Pentagon, the media, the American people and the peoples of other nations; the defendant Mr. Mark DeLouise, his family, his close associates and selectively his neighbors, depending on the frequency of his contacts with them; have all been subjected to intensive investigation with the use of highly sophisticated systems of surveillance. And, with all that, from then until now, the FBI has not found even one scintilla of evidence with which to incriminate my client. The defense will prove – with the prosecution's unintended, but unavoidable assistance – that Mark DeLouise is innocent of the government's charge of espionage, innocent beyond a shadow of a doubt."

When Leslie finished her opening statement, the courtroom was again briefly silent. Then the stirrings and whispered exchanges returned until Judge Simpson called for order and asked the prosecuting attorney to begin.

As I waited for Fischer to call her first witness, I was feeling confident. There was, after all, no incriminating evidence. How could the prosecution think it had a winnable case?

The first witness was "Gary Mengler." I did not recognize the name, but I did recognize his disturbingly familiar face. I whispered my concern to Leslie.

"That is one of the inmates who shouted racist insults at me during my first time in the slammer. I didn't see him there this time, so he must have been sent upstate."

"Hmm. Very interesting. I should have been informed of their intention to call this witness, but I'll leave it alone for now. I think he'll give me enough to take him and them down when I cross examine."

Leslie asked for a short recess. I had apprised her of my need for a restroom break, which others might welcome, too. More importantly, Leslie needed an opportunity to do a quick computer search on Mengler.

The recess gave me an opportunity to scan the faces of the spectators, as two guards escorted me toward a side door of the courtroom. It was reassuring to see Gracie's face in the crowd, looking strong and confident. I also appreciated seeing a few of our Westbeth neighbors, who had come to be in solidarity with me.

The guards returned me to the courtroom two or three minutes before the recess ended, time enough for Leslie to report the results of her computer search. Mr. Mengler had a twenty year sentence for robbery, rape, and attempted murder. It seemed logical that what he was about to present, as scripted for the purpose of my conviction, might earn him a reduced sentence, or at least more privileged conditions at whatever prison he was now being held. But Leslie was ready for him.

The court resumed session. Mengler took the stand. Fischer began her questions with confident assertion. Mengler responded by identifying me as his fellow inmate at the Metropolitan Correctional Center, claiming that he had had conversations with me in which I expressed hostility towards America. Mengler said,

"He was always bitchin' about our gover'ment an' criticizin' our military about things like Viet Nam and Panama. He even bad-mouthed General Colin Powell about Desert Stormin' Iraq, an' Colin Powell is black – an African-American, who he should be prouder of than I am."

"So how did that make you feel about Mr. DeLouise?"

"Well, it made me feel like he was sidin' with our enemies against his own country." Fischer was blatantly leading the witness. I looked at Leslie. Her returned expression assured me that she would be on top of this.

Fischer continued, "Mr. Mengler, when you heard that Mr. DeLouise had been charged with spying against the United States, did that seem to fit with some of the things you've told us?"

The question brought Leslie to her feet. She could wait no longer. "Objection, your Honor! That's leading the witness too far!"

"Sustained. Counselor, would you please rephrase the question?"

Fischer withdrew her question. As she returned to her seat, the court room buzzed with whispers, until there was a call for order. Then it was Leslie's turn to confront Mengler. Her face was stern. Although Mengler had put on a façade of smug confidence, he was clearly struck by Leslie's beauty and authority. He now slouched back in the witness chair.

"Mr Mengler," she began, you testified that you heard my client, Mr. DeLouise say unpatriotic things about America and its military. Is that correct?"

"Yeah. Yeah, tha's right."

"When and where did you hear him say those things?"

"Like I said – when we was in the Metropolitan Correctional Center."

"Yes, we know. But where in the Metropolitan Correctional Center? Under what circumstances? Was he speaking just to you or were others present?"

"Some other guys was there. They heard 'im, too."

"Where in the Center did you and 'some other guys' hear him say those things?"

"When we was eatin' or in the shower. Places like that."

"Mr. Mengler, do you know what solitary confinement is?"

Mengler acknowledged that he did.

"Well, Mr. Mengler, the only kind of imprisonment Mr. DeLouise has experienced at the Metropolitan Correctional Center is solitary confinement. That being the case, he was never able to speak with you or any other inmates. So he could not have said those things to you or to anyone else. Now, do you still want to claim that he did?"

Mengler was silent. Then he managed a feeble, "I got nothin' more t' say."

Her mission to discredit Mengler accomplished, Leslie graciously thanked him and turned to address the judge. "I have no further questions for this witness, your honor."

The prosecutor's eyes followed her failed witness disdainfully as he left the stand. She could not blame the failure all on Mengler, however, because she could not avoid her own failure to acknowledge the conditions of my incarceration. How could she have missed this? She turned her self-directed anger on Leslie, who had only done what any competent lawyer would do. Fischer would find a way to retaliate.

As the trial continued, Fischer's questioning of FBI agents Burns and Bennett produced little of use to the prosecution. Throughout their close surveillance of me, the FBI found no evidence to support the government's charge. Fischer's last witness, however, had knowledge of the secret military installation in question. Colonel Carrington would be able to relate my *Number 10* painting to the high security installation that supposedly was needed to defend America, and to argue that my ability to depict this facility could only mean my implication in a scheme of treason.

"Your Honor, the people call Colonel William F. Carrington to the stand."

Bill Carrington had come prepared to serve his country heroically. In dress uniform and impressively medaled, he strode, square-shouldered (although with a slight limp) to the witness stand.

In response to Fischer's questions, he related how he first came in contact with my *Number 10*, which, he stated was a depiction of a top-secret military building in actual existence, the location of which he could not reveal

Fischer continued her questions. "How then was Mr. DeLouise, a civilian, able to paint, in exact detail, a picture of that top-secret military building?"

"I don't really know for sure, counselor, but I think I have a theory."

"And what would that be, sir?"

"Well, I thought about the Rosenberg case and how easy it was for top-secret information to be taken from the Los Alamos atomic installation and passed on to those Communists. Unfortunately, in spite of our strict security measures, it's difficult to know who among our 'trusted' military, scientific and engineering personnel might be or decide to become a foreign agent."

"Is that to say you believe someone working in that building might be a foreign agent, and that such a person succeeded in getting photographic information to Mr. DeLouise?"

"That is correct."

"But why do it that way? Why not just send the information directly to Russia or China or whatever nation they were spying for?"

"We believe that the conspiracy against America is very broad. We believe that those involved in this plot wanted subversives from around the world to have access to these details – even other subversives right here in this country. This way, a subversive agent could go to the gallery, take pictures of the painting, and bring the information, safely stored in a camera, to some hostile group. Although publication of the painting is now forbidden, at first photographs of it were available to almost anyone who knew what magazine or paper to buy."

"I see. Then you think this may have been the way *Number 10* was played?"

"Yes, except that we haven't found the David Greenglass equivalent to help us solve this one."

"But you believe such a person really exists?"

"Yes, counselor, I do. How else could Mr. DeLouise have done the *Number 10* painting?"

Good question, Colonel. Thank you, sir. I have no further questions."

A brief recess was called before. Leslie began her cross-examination. As we waited, I reviewed in my mind the tragic history of the Rosenbergs. After my first detention, I had gone back to the library to better familiarize myself with their case. Greenglass, the brother of Ethel Rosenberg, was the key prosecution witness in the case against Julius and Ethel Rosenberg. His testimony, which many believe was perjured, led to the Rosenberg's execution. For the right wing, however, Greenglass was considered credible.

Now the court was called back to order and Leslie rose to the occasion, knowing that the Colonel's testimony would be taken seriously. To set him up, she began with disarmingly polite questions, aimed at his position and the role of the military. Perhaps, however, because at some level he doubted his own theory, he shifted restlessly.

"Colonel Carrington, how are you today, sir?"

"Oh, uh, fine, thank you."

"Are you still on active duty?"

"No. No, I'm not. I'm retired."

"What branch of the military were you in?"

"Army. I was in the field artillery."

Although the cross examination had not begun, beads of perspiration were already appearing on Bill Carrington's forehead.

"Colonel," she continued, "in terms of its competency, how would you rank U.S. military intelligence with that of other nations?"

"It's A-number-one. The best. And I'm not just saying that because I'm sitting here in this uniform."

Some of the spectators seemed amused, but the principal players in this courtroom drama either did not find the Colonel humorous or chose not to respond.

"Colonel, have you ever been inside the building alleged to be depicted in Mr. DeLouise's painting, *Number 10*?"

"No. I have not."

"Have you ever stood outside the building?"

"No. Never."

"Before your visit to Wesbeth Gallery with Agent Burns, had you ever seen an actual photograph of the building?"

"No."

"Then, Colonel, how can you say that a building you have never seen a photograph of, never entered into or stood outside of really exists?"

"Objection! Argumentative!"

"Sustained."

"I'll rephrase. Colonel Carrington, does the exact building alleged to be depicted in Mr. DeLouise's painting actually exist?"

Bill Carrington lowered his eyes to avoid Leslie's. As accustomed as he was to receiving unquestioning respect, he now wished that he could speak with more authority. He hesitated.

"I think so."

"Is that to say you don't really know, Colonel?"

"Objection! She's badgering the witness, your Honor."

"Overruled. Please answer the question, Colonel Carrington."

"Yes, that's right. I don't really know. I don't know because it's top-secret. There are those who could answer that question, but not me."

Leslie probably wondered why the prosecution had not brought in someone who had direct contact with this secret facility. She did not doubt that the facility existed, but the prosecution's choice not to bring in a direct witness was definitely to her advantage. She had no further questions for Carrington.

Perhaps not wanting to reveal the stress he felt as he was being cross-examined, the Colonel never wiped the sweat from his face while on the stand. As he walked away, slightly stoop-shouldered, with a now more discernable limp, he seemed to use his handkerchief more to hide than to combat the perspiration needing to be wiped from his face.

Leona Fischer was livid. Leslie had discredited two of the prosecution's witnesses. But I believed that there was more to her anger than that. As she turned her scowl in my direction, I wondered if she was thinking about my drawing of her bathroom, with the exact arrangement of its objects there-in, without my even knowing where she lived. I guessed that she must be trying to push this image away.

At first I hoped that Leona would say something that would

make this jury aware of the bathroom drawing. I realized, however, that it could not serve the interests of the prosecution. The drawing would only discredit Bill Carrington's theory. While thinking of this I again puzzled over the purpose of the drawing. Might the "force" use this in a dazzling entry, taking center stage in the courtroom drama? Knowing that this was most unlikely, my anxiety increased. Still, in my fantasy, I replayed my contacts with the little Orb and wished for its presence now.

It was Leslie's whispered, "Hey, where are you, Mark?" that brought me back to earth, just as Fischer was asking permission to approach the bench. After Judge Simpson heard her request, he called Leslie to share the decision.

As they talked, I could see anger in Leslie's expression. Leona Fischer left the discussion looking smug, while Leslie seemed to be muttering under her breath.

Judge Simpson then announced, "A matter of great importance to this case has come up, which requires testimony by a witness not present here today. Therefore, court is adjourned until 9:30 tomorrow morning."

The information relating to the new witness that Leslie shared with me and the other members of her defense team was a real set back. Leona Fischer was shuffling the prosecution's deck and getting ready to play her "win by any means necessary" card. For now, I will not share what Leslie knew. I will say only that whatever confidence I had in the obviousness of my innocence was gone. The little Orb had assured me that things would work out, but they were not working out now. I prayed to God for the strength to believe in the promise of my vindication.

As Leslie discussed our plan of defense, the jurors departed through a door leading back to the jury room; spectators wondered aloud about the new development; and the prosecution team began loading their files into expensive-looking attaché cases, as they shared opinions. The two guards waited impatiently for the session to close. Meanwhile, Gracie made her way over to me, pushing past Leslie and the others to give me a hug and the words, "I love you," that I so much needed to hear. Briefly, I held her close before the big, white, grim-faced guards moved toward us to cuff my hands and return me to my cell. I tried not to let Gracie see my pain, but it was there for her to see in my parting smile and hear in my voice.

"Don't worry, Gracie. Believe in the promise of the little Orb. Believe that God's plan demands my vindication. And tell Sarah to keep the faith."

As I was being escorted away, I appreciated seeing Gracie and Leslie embrace, then walk toward the exit in serious discussion.

On my way back to prison, I thought about what Leslie's assisting defense attorneys might be thinking. They could not understand what was happening the way that Leslie and I did, because they could not know about the "force." They did, however, know about the drawing of Fischer's bathroom. Although we could not yet give them direct information about my extra-terrestrial contacts, they must have had fantasies. Clearly, they did not share the prosecution's need to deny the mysterious nature of the connection between the drawing and my *Number 10*.

Chapter 17

THE FRAME-UP

B ack in my cell, I was comforted by the promise of the "force."
Leslie believed that a frame-up was in the works, but I wanted
to trust that there was a plan to exonerate me. That I had "nothing to
fear" was a thought that entered my mind like a mantra. The mantras
became preludes to prayer. I believed the "force" to be an agent of
a higher power, but fallible. But because "God" seemed so abstract
and unknowable, I looked for concrete reassurance. I needed human
contact, or perhaps communication from the little Orb. As I thought
of the little Orb, I got an immediate response.

"I am here! Just wait."

To wait was all that I could possibly do. And waiting brought
to mind America's political victims. Innocent victims like the
Rosenbergs, and Sacco and Vanzetti before them, became targets
for blame because of their politics, and were executed in spite of
public protests. As I hoped for alien intervention, I reminded myself
that these martyrs also deserved intervention. My case, however,
was different, because it was the aliens who had gotten me into this
trouble in the first place. They had a responsibility to get me out – and
Vladimir as well. I prayed for my vindication and gave thanks for my
unexplainable extraterrestrial support. I did appreciate my privilege.

I thought also of Mumia Abu Jamal, imprisoned in Pennsylvania since 1982. On testimony which contradicted the evidence, Mumia was convicted of murdering a policeman. Even with further evidence of his innocence, his conviction still stands. From his prison cell, he continues to write with intelligence and passion, protesting oppression and supporting resistance. Because of this, he receives international support; which has not brought about his release, but has at least, so far, kept him alive.

As I thought about how my painting of *Number 10* led to my arrest, it seemed logical that some equally mysterious event might bring about my liberation. Almost as a game, I entertained ridiculous fantasies: For example, I imagined me and my family beamed out of New York by the "force," landing safely in some Utopian place. I had to laugh, and as I did, I could have sworn that I heard distant laughter joining mine.

The rest of the day was spent routinely. Night brought restless intermittent sleep and nightmarish thoughts. I expected my conviction soon. Seeing Gracie again would help renew my courage. Leslie would do her best, but the "justice" system had its agenda. I would have to be punished. My conviction would be a warning to all dissident artists.

And, in truth, I was the agent of a foreign power – beyond foreign, an extraterrestrial power, something a jury would not understand. I knew very little about this power, but what I did know was awesome. Such a power might have given me unwavering confidence, but I needed and sought greater assurance. I needed to connect with the sacred, to somehow see a concrete manifestation of the spirit. Gracie's confident smile helped. I would be looking for her smile as soon as I returned to court.

After breakfast, the guards put me in a van for the trip back to court. As we approached the building, I was again aware of the crowds. Pro and con, the public was still involved in my case. Their loud rhythmic chants and shouts must have been heard for blocks. Police held back the crowds, and held back photographers and reporters as well, so that court participants could move freely up the steps and through the doors. As they did, cameras clicked and reporters shouted questions. Passing by this confusion, we arrived at the back of the courthouse, where the same two tough guards were waiting to escort me in.

In the courtroom, the only people present were attorneys, witnesses, and the military and government personnel I had spotted earlier. Spectators had not yet been admitted, and only after they were, would the jury be filing in. Leslie and her team and I greeted each other, and sat down at our table together to review our defense against the prosecution's final offensive.

At 9:15, the court stenographer entered and set up her stenotype machine. About five minutes later, the doors were opened, admitting the stream of best-seat-seeking spectators. I looked for Gracie. Our eyes met. We smiled. Then Gracie took a seat on the defense side, in the first row, as close to me as possible. Her being able to be that close seemed like a sign. Eventually, we would be back together, but I could not know how long that would be.

After the judge and jury entry, the attorneys were called to the back for instruction. Then they returned to their respective areas to confer with their associates and check their notes for the final battle. A few coughs and throat-clearings interrupted the silence, as all awaited the opening words. Leona Fischer began.

Your honor, the people call Mr. Milton Travis to the stand."

I took a good look at Milton Travis as he walked toward the stand. I was certain that I had never seen him before. Just how would this man testify against me? The man was, I guessed, in his mid-forties. He was a fair-skinned Caucasian of medium height and build. He had large ears, an aquiline nose, and light brown hair, thinning slightly at the crown. His thick eyebrows stood out over heavy-lidded cold blue eyes, and his thin lips seemed almost lost in his thick moustache and Vandyke beard. He was smartly attired.

He looked straight at me, in a manner that suggested that I had been identified for him at some earlier time. Then, with his hand on the Bible, he took the oath – "to tell the truth, the whole truth and nothing but the truth, so help me God." I sat back and waited for the inevitable charade of lies.

"Mr. Travis, would you please tell the court what kind of work you do."

"I'm an electrical engineer."

"Maybe some of us don't fully understand what an electrical engineer does, Mr. Travis. Please explain."

"I'm involved in the practical application of the theory of electricity to the construction of electrically powered machinery."

"I see. And where do you work?"

"Uh, well, I'm presently unemployed."

"Then where did you work?"

"At a U.S. military installation."

"As a civilian employee? Or are you in the military service?"

"I have been in the military, but I was a civilian employee with special security clearance."

"So what happened? Why did you leave this job?"

Clearly, this all had been rehearsed. Travis had been well briefed, instructed and coached. I shared my thoughts with Leslie, who smiled sardonically, and nodded, as Travis responded.

"I had no choice. I was forced to leave."

"And why was that?"

"I betrayed a trust. It finally caught up with me."

"Tell us what this was. In what way did you betray trust?"

Travis was playing his role to the hilt – the shame-faced look, the nervous shift. "I foolishly got involved," he began, hesitating dramatically, "in a terrible conspiracy – a conspiracy to spy against my country."

"What made you decide to do such a thing?"

"Greed, I guess. I wanted the money. It seemed like an opportunity to make more money in one lump sum than I could ever hope to make in my entire life."

"What else do you want to tell us about that today, Mr. Travis?"

"I am so ashamed. It was so wrong. And when the FBI caught up with me ten days ago, I knew what I was facing and what I had to do. I got to thinking (since I've been following the case), that I should do whatever I can to help you here. I can't undo my mistake, but I can at least tell you what I know. There is no way that this other guy should go free, while I spend the rest of my life in prison, away from my wife and three kids – or worse."

"This 'other guy.' To whom were you referring?"

"The man who was in on it with me. The painter. I gave him the pictures I took of the center, and he did the painting."

"And do you now see this man anywhere in the courtroom?"

I tensed, as he turned and pointed his finger at me.

"Let the record show," Fisher continued, that the witness has identified the defendant, Mark DeLouise, as his accomplice in the crime of espionage against the United States, for the benefit of a foreign nation or nations. No further questions, your honor."

A murmur arose from among the spectators, causing the judge to call for order. Leslie asked to approach the bench. Permission was granted, and Judge Simpson signaled the prosecutor to join them. Leslie requested time to consult with her client and her associate attorneys. The judge and prosecutor agreed to allow this, and the judge called a thirty minute recess to clear the court.

Leslie asked Gracie to join us while she and her associates tried to assess our situation. I found it difficult to concentrate on their legal jargon. Instead, I was torn between a longing to hold my wife and a gnawing concern over the absence of the little Orb. Here I was, facing the probability of being found guilty of a crime that never happened. Where was the "force," the power that had gotten me into this mess?

Leslie's next communication brought my focus back with a jolt: "Mark, I think we may have to put you on the stand."

Yes, I admonished myself – I did need to be fully involved in this strategy discussion. Gracie must have known that she herself was a distraction. And she also knew what else was on my mind.

"Our friends up there will come through for you." Touching my hand, she added, "We all believe that God has a plan for you. We do not know how this trial will come out, but, soon or later, you will be vindicated."

While "later" was not what I hoped for, Gracie's calm courage was reassuring. Perhaps Leslie invited Gracie to join us, expecting that she might say what I needed to hear.

Leslie then went on to explain that the final decision for me to take the stand was contingent on what happened in her cross-examination. If she could expose the contradictions in his testimony, Travis's perjury should be obvious. Then I should not need to testify, and I could thus avoid the prosecution's cross-examination. Leslie's fear was that Fischer might use my grand jury response relating to how I got the information to paint *Number 10*. ("Through a source that comes from far beyond this world," I had explained.) She would suggest that I had made up some UFO story to protect my "co-conspirators." The bathroom drawing, of course, was evidence that something far more mysterious was involved. Leslie, however, could not bring this in unless Fischer did, and that was not about to happen.

"The illogic of Travis's testimony should be obvious to any intelligent person," Leslie observed, "but if I have any ability for picking up how a jury is responding, I have to say that this one seems to be buying Travis's story."

Chapter 18

* ———— ✦ ———— *

THE DEFENSE

The recess was now ended. The court was called back into session, and Judge Simpson asked Leslie if she was ready to cross-examine the witness.

"Yes, your honor. The defense calls Mr. Milton Travis to the stand."

Travis, from where he had been positioned in the courtroom, had not our view of the jury. Even if he had more opportunity to "read" the jury, I doubt that he would have picked up the cues of their credulity. He seemed worried – perhaps responding to some discomfort with his own lies, although he may have convinced himself that they served patriotic cause, beyond whatever more tangible incentive the prosecution must have offered him. Leslie's intimidating presence added to his worry. In spite of her concerns, she did not let them undermine her confrontational confidence.

As I watched him shift uncomfortably in the witness box, I tried to calm my own anxiety. When would I be rescued? Why had the little orbicular messenger made no timely appearance to bring us clues and cues? I had to remind myself that I was chosen for a special purpose. Knowing that Vladimir was playing my same role half way around the world, I had to believe that, whatever the mysterious plan, our task was critical. It seemed that Vladimir and I were agents of the "force," serving the galaxy. For me, prayer helped, and I assumed that Vladimir also had some source of strength. I wondered about the developments in Vladimir's case, but my focus now was Leslie's cross-examination of Travis. I settled back in my chair as she began.

"Mr. Travis, you testified that you took pictures of a top-secret military center and gave them to 'the painter.' Did you forget his name?"

"No. I didn't forget. His name is Mark – Mark DeLouise."

"How long have you known Mr. DeLouise?"

"Just long enough to deliver the pictures to him."

"And when was that?"

"Sometime in April. I'm not sure of the exact day."

"Do you remember the time of day?"

"It was in the evening, around 10."

"And where did you deliver the pictures?"

"I took them to a building called Westbeth, located in the West Village, where Mr. DeLouise lives. It was all arranged."

"All arranged by whom?"

"The man who contacted me. He called himself 'Sakharov.' That was the only name I knew him by."

"When and where did Sakharov contact you, Mr. Travis?"

"Last year, around the end of May. I went to the 42nd Street Library to do some research. He came to the table where I was reading, sat next to me and said, 'Hello, Mr. Travis. I was startled by this total stranger with a foreign accent, who knew my name. He introduced himself simply as 'Sakharov,' then, without hesitation, made his proposition."

"And did you ask Mr. Sakharov how he knew who you were, and how he managed to find you at the library?"

"Yes, of course. I now believe that it was all set up by the KGB. They must have already checked me out and then checked out DeLouise, and then tracked me until I stopped at a place where there could be easy contact. That place just happened to be the 42nd Street Library."

"Now, Mr. Travis, would you please tell us about Mr. Sakharov's proposition."

"Well, first of all, he told me that his mission was in the interest of gaining world peace. America, he pointed out, is determined to remain the dominant global military power. Even though there does not now seem to be any threat from Communism, there are people in the world with ideas which threaten American freedom. So the U.S. must stay ahead in its nuclear arms capacity. While it continues to produce and test more efficient weapons, other nations would like to do the same. The tensions created by this situation, according to him, could lead to World War III and the extinction of all higher life forms, including, of course humans. The best way to prevent this destruction would be world disarmament, which could begin with internationally balanced power. Exposing America's military secrets could lead to this balance of power."

"Apparently Russia's military secrets have also been exposed. Why, Mr. Travis, do you think that the KGB would want the military secrets of its own nation exposed?"

"I don't know. I believed Sakharov to be Russian, but perhaps he was not KGB. Maybe he represented some group that was trying to bring back Communism. I let myself believe that helping to expose the U.S. secrets would be a good thing, but I admit that perhaps the real reason was because Sakharov offered me a lot of money. America is the best country in the world. It is essential to defend it, but when he said that he had already met with Mark DeLouise at Westbeth, and that DeLouise agreed to co-operate for a payment of two and one half million dollars, I found it hard to resist."

"So how did you go about helping to expose these secrets?"

"I bought two new cameras, a speed graphic and a reflex, to make sure I got the best results. I took pictures of the exterior and interior features in the high security building where I worked, and then delivered them to DeLouise in the Westbeth Gallery."

"Recall for us if you will, Mr. Travis, your visit to Westbeth. On what floor is the gallery?"

"On the second floor. But I could be wrong. It's been a good while since I went there."

"Is it something you would forget.? Do you remember whether you took the stairs or the elevator to get there?"

"No, I don't. Not really. I visit quite a few galleries, so it's hard to keep track of how they're situated."

"Well, you wouldn't have had to take either one, Mr. Travis. The Westbeth Gallery is on the ground floor."

If Travis was going to be a convincing witness for the prosecution, he should have been better instructed. It was good that he wasn't, but it may not have made a difference. I looked for some expression of doubt among the jurors, but I didn't see it. They may have already made up their minds against me.

Leslie was now pursuing the credibility of what Travis claimed were necessary steps. Travis explained that he had done his own processing in his apartment, in order to protect his secret. He had not chosen digital technology because he felt that using his computer would make his action less secure. Sakharov, he claimed, had wanted DeLouise to do the painting from the photos, and then wanted new photos made from the painting. The new film would remain in the camera to be carried, presumably, to Russia. His narrative seemed incredibly contrived. I wondered how a jury could take it seriously, but still feared that they would.

"Was processing the films really necessary? Couldn't you have just left them in the cameras from the beginning and given them to Sakharov?"

"No. Sakharov demanded proof of my work."

As I was wondering where Leslie would go from here, I overheard the voice of the little Orb, speaking to her.

"Ask the witness about microfilm."

Microfilm seemed like a more practical choice. Leslie proceeded to establish Travis's familiarity with the technology and its suitability for his project. Travis explained quite competently that microfilm could be stored in very small space and then viewed in its original size by means of a special viewer. Prints 8"x10" or larger could be produced from it in either color or black and white.

"Considering what you just told us about the uses of microfilm," she asked, "why was the painting necessary?"

Travis could only say that that was what Sakharov wanted. I recalled that when Bill Carrington had been questioned, he had at least come up with a logical explanation for the painting. Having the work publicly displayed, Carrington had explained, made it available to a significant number of subversive operatives, from both within and outside of the United States. Travis, however, had probably been advised to focus more on the "service to a foreign nation" charge, even though it could not make sense.

He then went on to say that he had not been paid the promised two and one half million dollars, which made him feel that he had "been had."

There was good reason to believe, however, that Travis would receive a substantial sum of money for framing me.

Knowing that Travis would misunderstand her reference, Leslie then asked how lying made him feel.

"Furious," he responded, "at him and at myself, for buying his lies and betraying my country. I wish I could get my hands on him."

Leslie clarified her question. "No, I meant you, Mr. Travis. How does it feel to sit there and lie to this court?"

"Objection! Unwarranted accusation!"

Sustained. Careful, Ms. Chen."

"I have no further questions for this witness, your honor."

"Alright, then. You may step down, Mr. Travis."

In examining Travis, Fischer had not pushed him past his own confession, and identification of me as his accomplice, because she had counted on Leslie bringing out more of his story during the cross-examination. She had counted right, but she had not counted on Leslie directing attention to the illogic of his story. By confronting the issue of Travis's lies, Leslie was hoping to reinforce what should have already been obvious. And while the judge, as expected, sustained the prosecutor's objection to Leslie's accusation, the thought was still out there and had not even been stricken from the record.

While it would have been good for the jury to see me as a "real person," Leslie continued to fear what might happen in a cross-examination. She decided, therefore, to let Travis's story stand, without my refutation, hoping that the jury would see how improbable it was. Instead, she brought in two witnesses to speak for my character – Dr. Janet Weich, psychiatric unit chief at Meredith General where I had worked and Rev. Jim Daniels, pastor of our church. They both testified as to my integrity. They pointed out that my protests of American injustice were aimed at healing, not harm.

With no further witnesses to testify, the prosecution and defense rested.

Chapter 19

* ———————⊛——————— *

SUMMATION

Judge Simpson then called on both sides to make their closing statements. Leona Fischer wore a look of exasperation. She knew that her last witness had not responded well to Leslie's cross-examination, but hoped that the jury would choose to believe him anyway. Taking on a look of confidence, she aimed at effective argument through use of pretentious language, rather than substance.

"Ladies and gentlemen of the jury, I noted with great appreciation your diligent attention to the evidentiary details of the people's case against the defendant, Mr. Mark DeLouise, on trial here for the crime of espionage in service to a foreign nation, against the United States of America. His defense, as to be expected, spared no attempt at chicanery to undermine the witnesses who have testified against him. Those who testified in their belief in his 'good character,' I fear are themselves deceived, but I trust that your study of this case will lead you to a different conclusion. Insight and critical thought can attune you to the DeLouise crime that may threaten our national security. Let us review some of the more salient facts which point most convincingly to the guilt of Mr. DeLouise.

Fischer continued with well-practiced dramatic measures, directed for optimum persuasion.

"Although the *Number 10* painting made by Mr. DeLouise

was on public view for several weeks, its showing is now banned in the interest of national security. Since its Westbeth showing, authorities were able to verify the source of the information it depicts (information which has been classified as top secret) and have been doing everything possible to prevent its further exposure, including the censoring of material already published. For this reason, you have not been able to actually see the painting. Instead, we have the sworn testimony of two very reliable witnesses, that they viewed the painting together in the presence of Mr. DeLouise while it was exhibited at the Westbeth Gallery. Agent Daniel Burns of the Federal Bureau of Investigation and Colonel William F. Carrington (retired) of the U.S. Army originally had their suspicions and initiated the investigation which has led to this trial. They could see no legitimate source for access to the information he depicts, and, therefore, assumed that the source was a betrayal from within, a theory now verified by the testimony of Mr. Travis.

For those who know the work of Mr. DeLouise, his co-operation with a foreign agent comes as no surprise. Many of his paintings and drawings are critical of our nation's domestic and international policies and image, while others glorify communism in Cuba and the struggles of insurgent forces in other parts of Latin America. Such creations show little loyalty to this nation in which he has acquired an excellent college education, membership in a prestigious health profession, and access to amenities which are the envy of many around the world who do not share his privilege of American citizenship.

The defense, of course, doesn't want you to believe the testimony of Mr. Milton Travis, who gave us his sworn account of the espionage arrangement which, he states, brought him and Mr. DeLouise together as co-conspirators. Mr. Travis explained how top-secret U.S. military information was photographed, processed and painted in meticulous detail for convenient photographing by a foreign agent, to be stolen out of our country concealed in cameras, and delivered to theirs.

What does the defense expect you to believe? That Mr. DeLouise's meticulously accurate painting of a top-secret U.S. military building and its intricate interior installations were inspired by some sort of artistic dream? Ladies and gentlemen, based on the evidence testified to here, and the impossibility of his having acquired the information to create this painting in any other way, I call on you to find the defendant Mark DeLouise, guilty as charged."

Some in the jury had seemed spellbound as they listened to Leona Fischer's scathing remarks, but Leslie's wit and words were honed to counter any spell. Leslie had crafted what I hoped would be a persuasive-enough call for my acquittal.

"Ladies and gentlemen of the jury, while there is nothing else stated in this case with which the prosecutor and I agree, I stand with her in greatly appreciating your earnest attention to the testimonies – the illogic of which should make clear the fallacious nature of the charge against my client, Mark DeLouise.

First, we heard Gary Mengler's testimony in which he claimed to have heard my client say things in places where they could never have been together at the Metropolitan Correctional Center. We know that these conversations never occurred, because my client was always kept in solitary confinement, away from fellow inmates. Nor were we presented with any evidence, not even by Colonel Carrington, that this "secret building" actually exists. Then Milton Travis tells a tale of photographing this mysterious building and delivering the photos to my client at the Westbeth Gallery. The alleged plan for delivering the secrets to the enemy defies all logic. We must question whether or not Mr. Travis ever met the accused or was at the gallery. When asked about the gallery's location, he did not know what floor it was on – a detail someone in his profession on a special espionage mission would be expected to retain.

The witnesses against Mr. DeLouise either lacked convicting information or related stories that were blatantly false, or seemed not logically true. The FBI, represented by Agent Daniel Burns, in spite of close surveillance and intensive investigation, was unable to find a scintilla of evidence to justify the prosecution's charge against Mr. Delouise.

As for the prosecution's claim that my client's protest art is un-American, you heard two distinguished character witnesses, a pastor and a psychiatrist who both know him and his work well, point out that, far from showing a disloyalty, his creative work is aimed at turning our country toward healing itself. His art has always been exhibited openly for everyone to see, to learn from, to be inspired by, to enjoy, or to criticize. They both testified as to the high esteem in which they and so many others hold him; about his dedication to his patients; his team spirit at work; and his veracity.

Admittedly, my client's painting is a puzzle. But if you are inclined to believe the prosecution's theory of espionage, let me remind you of the public knowledge that we are all aware of. We know the story of Vladimir Ivanov, who, like my client, has been charged with espionage for painting a top secret military installation. But Ivanov lives in Russia and has been charged by the Russian government. Mr. Travis, the surprise witness for the prosecution, claims that *my* client was working with a Russian agent, and spying for Russia. If this had been so, why would the Russian artist now be held by his government on similar charges? Col. Carrington has suggested that the enemy here is not a 'foreign nation,' but rather an international conspiracy. If this is true (and there is no evidence to support it), my client might be guilty of something, but not of the charge for which he is now on trial.

Whatever differences you may have with the politics of Mr. DeLouise, there is no credible evidence connecting him to the alleged betrayal. And certainly, even if you are inclined to believe Travis's story, does not the arrest of Mr. Ivanov create reasonable doubt? What we have heard here must bring us to the only conclusion justice can abide: your verdict that Mark DeLouise is not guilty."

As Leslie was delivering her closing statement, I studied the jurors' faces. What I saw was a mixed bag of yes, no and maybe expressions. I could not imagine what their final decision would be. The testimony of the key witness for the prosecution should have been understood as clearly illogical, but then my story could not have made sense to them either. With no discernible logic on either side, would the jury find "reasonable doubt?"

All I could do was hope and pray. I turned around to catch Gracie's supportive expression. Whatever the outcome of this trial, we knew that eventually I would be vindicated. Leslie returned to our table, sat down beside me, and touched my hand. Judge Simpson called for order.

"Ladies and gentlemen of the jury: it is your honorable duty in this case to decide the guilt or innocence of the defendant, Mark DeLouise. Before reaching your decision, it is important that you weigh very carefully all of the evidence that has been presented to you here. The defendant, Mark DeLouise, has been accused of the crime of espionage against the United States of America, for the benefit of a foreign nation. You must bear in mind that no one may be convicted of a crime unless there is proof beyond a reasonable doubt that he has committed the crime for which he is charged. In order to return a verdict of guilty in this case, each one of you must be convinced that:

A. Mark DeLouise entered into a conspiracy with Milton Travis, a witness for the prosecution, who so testified, and a foreign agent named by that witness, to commit the crime of espionage against the United States of America for the benefit of a foreign nation.

B. And that being offered by said foreign agent a payment of two and one half million dollars, Mark DeLouise agreed to paint and did in fact paint and exhibit publicly the exact depiction of a photograph taken by Milton Travis of the exterior and interior details of a top security U.S. military building for the purpose of espionage.

If you find after you have thoroughly weighed all of the evidence that the charge brought against the defendant Mark DeLouise is true, you may find him guilty. The penalty for such a crime may be as severe as death; but may be limited to imprisonment for life without parole. The court will consider the jury's recommendation of the sentence it believes is warranted. In accordance with federal law, the jury's verdict for such a case must be unanimous. When you withdraw to begin your deliberations, please select one of your members to preside and speak on your behalf. If necessary, you may call upon the court for a re-reading of testimony about which you have questions. You must notify me immediately when you have reached a verdict. If you find that much more time is needed for your deliberations, arrangements have been made to have you sequestered, and you will be informed of the details relating to this. Thank you."

Whatever fears there were among the jurors for American security, I did not see how they could believe that I was in league with a "foreign nation" – not with the parallel arrest of Vladimir Ivanov, a citizen of the nation in question. But it was difficult to imagine what kind of fantasies might be running through the minds of those whose patriotism was built on paranoia and chauvinism. Perhaps there would at least be enough rational jurors to bring about a deadlock, even if the illogic of my own story was a problem. Leslie commented that a guilty verdict would "fly in the face" of reasonable doubt, but there was no guarantee of reason.

The jury, as expected, did need to be sequestered. On the afternoon of the fourth day, we were called back to court. A verdict had been reached.

Chapter 20

* ———————⊕———————— *

THE VERDICT AND
SENTENCE

There was silence in the courtroom. The hush that comes with anticipation – with wishing, with fear, and for some of us, prayer. Judge Simpson was about to read the paper handed him on which my immediate fate was written. I saw what I thought might be a hint of disappointment on his face. I braced myself for the worst.

"Will the defendant please rise."

Catching Leslie's expression, I assumed that she also had picked up on the judge's reaction. As we stood to hear the verdict, we exchanged glances.

"How does the jury find?"

As I awaited the response, I had to remind myself that, however long my vindication might be delayed, I had to keep the faith. The foreman then read the expected verdict.

"For the crime of espionage against the United States of America, for the benefit of a foreign nation, we the jury find the defendant Mark DeLouise guilty as charged."

The courtroom exploded. Those who agreed with the verdict congratulated themselves quietly, but those who understood how wrong the verdict was, shouted their anger loudly. Judge Simpson gaveled for order. Reporters scurried off, presumably to retrieve their cell phones from security and relay the news, and then to wait for jurors and witnesses to interview. I imagined that outside, cameras were flashing and video crews hustling.

Leslie reached out to touch my shoulder. Gracie headed toward me. The guards quickly moved Gracie and Leslie aside, positioning themselves at my left and my right, while the judge confirmed the verdict.

"Mr. Mark DeLouise, a jury of your peers has found you guilty as charged, of the crime of espionage against the United States of America for the benefit of a foreign nation. You are, therefore, remanded to custody at the Metropolitan Correctional Center, where you will remain until your return to this court for sentencing at nine a.m. on Monday, March 29, 1999. Thank you, ladies and gentlemen of the jury, for your diligence in hearing this case, and for your earnest deliberations to reach a verdict. Your accompanying recommendation will be taken into consideration."

The recommendation concerned the sentence, the severity of which – depending on how the judge decided – we wouldn't know for two months. After ordering everyone else to be seated, the judge dismissed the jurors, so they could collect their belongings and leave ahead of the spectators. Then he instructed the guards to take me away. I turned my head for one last look at Gracie.

Back in my prison cell, my promised rescue seemed further and further off. As I began to struggle against a sense of panic, I had to remind myself that the "force" had a plan. Mine was not an ordinary wrongful conviction. Unlike other innocents who had been imprisoned (some even executed), I had been put in this situation by extra-terrestrials. They got me into this, and they had the power to get me (and Vladimir) out. But how long would it take? As I thought of the two long months ahead, especially of the separation from my family, anger welled up inside of me.

Yet I realized that it often took high-profile victims to wake people up. I thought about Mumia Abu Jamal, still in prison. I thought about those who had been killed by police, like Anthony

Baez and Amadou Diallo. Unlike them, I would be rescued. I waited for reassurance from the "force."

Then, perhaps in response to the demanding vibrations of my thoughts, the little Orb appeared in my cell. My return to prison, the little Orb explained, was a necessary part of the plan. I would be able to continue telepathic communication with my family and Leslie.

As the days dragged by, Gracie did keep me informed telepathically. She kept me abreast, locally and globally, of the most urgent issues, including, of course, what the establishment media was saying about me and Vladimir. We had known that Vladimir had also been found guilty, but what came as a shock was his sentencing date. Although New York and Moscow times differ by eight hours, we were sentenced at exactly the same moment: March 29, 1999 – I at nine a.m., and he at five p.m.

Vladimir and I resumed telepathic communication, commiserating with each other. We fantasized our longed-for day of liberation, when we hoped to bring our families together for celebration.

The prison visits were few, and separated by a thick plate glass window. What we really wanted most was to be with each other close enough to touch. Nevertheless, the visits, along with our telepathic talks, helped me to bear the slow passage of time.

From Gracie's telepathic updates, I learned about support for Vladimir in Russia, and the continuing demonstrations, marches and fundraising events for me here. Gracie participated in many of these events, but chose not to take the speaker role. Sarah was anxious to go to the events, usually with her mother, but sometimes with friends.

If our supporters, or even those who demonstrated against us, had any notion of my extra-terrestrial connection, I wondered how this knowledge would have changed the drama that was being played out in my defense. If they even believed in intelligent life elsewhere in the galaxy, their trust or distrust in such life would have been critical. With this knowledge, organizing for street action might have given way to confusion, and for some, wonderment.

Gracie continued to provide me with telepathic news reports, but wasted little time on such distractions as the Monica Lewinsky escapade. The attack on the Balkans was a more serious matter. Employing the rhetoric of "humanitarian intervention," Washington had organized its military might to control the former Yugoslavia, the strategic pathway from the oil rich areas of South Asia to Western Europe. While the imperialist agenda of the U.S. (and Germany) had been clear to us for some time, most Americans had no understanding of how investments of American finance capital had unloosed forces of nationalism in the Balkans. While Gracie and her friends were out in the streets protesting the war, the most dedicated crowds found baseball more important.

The days passed slowly by, until at last it was Monday, March 29 – sentencing day. While I was being transported to the courthouse in the prison van, I heard the familiar rhythmic chants of my supporters grow louder and louder. The words of the protesters increasingly reflected the understanding that I was tied to other political prisoners, and to the struggle for justice everywhere.

"Free Mark DeLouise, free Mumia, free Leonard Peltier and all political prisoners! Jobs, not jails. Stop police brutality. Money for human needs, not for bombs!"

Flanked by two hefty guards, I entered the courtroom at 8:50 a.m. Spectators. press corps, prosecution and defense teams, and, of course, Gracie, awaited me. A guard removed my handcuffs.

Gracie had been able to secure an almost front row seat, to my right rear, where I could turn my head to see her and exchange looks. Although I was about to be sentenced, I knew, as did Vladimir and the few who were close to us, that the extra-terrestrial plan would supercede state power. Believing this, our smiles for each other held our anticipation of my eventual vindication and freedom.

"All rise," brought us to our feet. With customary solemnity, Judge Simpson entered and ordered us to be seated. His look at me telegraphed his fateful words to come. Clearing his throat, he turned to address the court.

"Ladies and gentlemen, the pursuit of justice can be a daunting or courageous one, depending on the nature of the case brought before it. There are those special cases when mixed emotions are felt.

I believe this has been such a case. As judge, I endeavor to hold in check any emotion which might unduly affect my impartiality. Now that the evidence has been presented, the testimonies and arguments heard, and the verdict reached; I must pronounce a judgment based on the verdict, the law, and the recommendation of the jury."

Ordering me to stand, he looked authoritatively at me; as what seemed to be a glimmer of compassion was quickly suppressed.

"Mark DeLouise, you have been found guilty in this court by a jury of your peers, of the crime of espionage against your country, the United States of America, for the benefit of a foreign nation. It is now my painful duty to pronounce that you be sentenced to life imprisonment without parole, as recommended by the jury."

Gasps ran through the courtroom. Simpson gaveled for order and then continued.

"The crime is one which on the scale of justice, far outweighs the crime of premeditated murder of an individual. The deliberate passing of classified military information to a foreign nation, whether or not hostile, holds the potential to cause, with or without warning, the violent deaths of thousands, hundreds of thousands, perhaps even millions of innocent people and the destruction of infrastructure and life-sustaining resources. For such a crime, you are sentenced to life imprisonment without parole."

The repeated order of my sentence brought further bursts of reaction. How could I have threatened such danger when there seemed to be no "foreign nation" with which I was in league? As if to keep back the contradiction, the judge gaveled more insistently still. Then he continued.

"You will be taken from here to the Metropolitan Correctional Center to begin the transfer to Sing Sing Maximum Security Correctional Facility. Before leaving the Metropolitan Correctional Center, you will be permitted to meet with your family and your attorney, who presumably intends to appeal."

As the judge finished this final instruction, the stir and murmur of the spectators resumed. He then asked,

"Is there anything you would like to say before you leave, Mr. DeLouise?"

Mentally, in anticipation of an opportunity to speak, I had already rehearsed a statement. As I began, I fortified myself, hoping that the press would seriously acknowledge my veracity.

"Yes, your honor. I do have something to say. In spite of the fact that in my creative statements as a visual artist I have protested the many injustices which characterize America; and I have sought to expose how American imperialism leads to war; I am innocent of the crime of espionage against the United States of America for the benefit of a foreign nation. My goal has always been to heal the nation and the world. And with the help of God, my exceptionally competent attorney, my loving family, and loyal friends; I will prove my innocence beyond a shadow of a doubt. As part of their scheme to incriminate me, the prosecution deliberately procured two witnesses for the purpose of giving false testimony. This scheme will be exposed, and I will be free."

The response of cheers and applause demonstrated clearly that the majority of the courtroom spectators were my supporters. The judge gaveled for order, and signaled the guards to quickly take me out. Summarily, he dismissed the court. I shared a parting look with Gracie, and looked forward to her anticipated brief visit before I would be sent upstate. I was prepared to go the next round.

Gracie and Leslie were at the Metropolitan Correctional Center a few minutes after my arrival there. They explained that they had been met by four police officers who escorted them through the surging crowd of reporters and onlookers to a waiting squad car which brought them to the prison. Thankfully, we were able to speak without the separation of the thick glass window or a steel mesh screen, but my hands were still cuffed behind my back. It might be a long time before we saw each other again. I needed so much to share a good tight hug.

We agreed on how we would proceed. We would reassure Sarah that everything was going to work out. Gracie would call both her parents and mine, assuring them that we had connections in "high places" that would prove my innocence. They would, of course, assume that "high places" referred to some American political influence. Leslie's talk about how appealing the verdict was a ploy to hold media attention, and an imperative in our effort to expose the corrupt prosecution. For the sake of all the wrongly convicted, the wall of injustice had to be exposed, regardless of my expected liberation by the "force."

Chapter 21

PRISON "BREAKS"

Several weeks went by (six to be exact) after my arrival at Sing Sing, and I had not seen or heard from the little Orb. I was more than just a little concerned, but decided it was too soon to lose patience. After all, it was only six weeks, not six months, or God forbid, six years.

Except for some telepathic contact, I had missed Mother's Day with Gracie and Sarah. Father's Day and my birthday were coming up soon, and we would all be thankful for our telepathy. But because my freedom was not at hand, I needed to hear something from the "force." What was the game plan for my release? Why did I have to wait so long for contact from the little Orb? I had to reassure myself that I was important to the "force," and hope that I would not have to wait much longer. Meanwhile, my best "escape" from prison was my ability to communicate with Gracie and Sarah telepathically. We invited Leslie to join us when any *ex post facto* questions crept into our discussions of my case. It was during one of these discussions that Leslie brought up the history of the Rosenbergs.

"Mark, how does it feel to be in the same prison where the Rosenbergs spent their last days and were executed?"

"I feel comradeship." My answer was without hesitation. Like me, Julius and Ethel Rosenberg had been victims of a political agenda.

Although their execution had been generations ago, the Rosenbergs were a frequent reference at the anti-death penalty protests which I supported. We in our anti-death penalty movement believed that they were innocent of espionage, but that their deaths served the agenda of anti-Communism.

Before I was accused of the same crime, I had read two accounts of their involvement in the alleged Los Alamos spy operation; their investigation by the FBI; and their trial, conviction, imprisonment and execution. Through these accounts, I felt some familiarity with the Rosenbergs and the two authors who told their story. One account was *The Implosion Conspiracy*, by Louis Nizer. I was impressed with Nizer's research, but he seemed not to understand the political machinations of the FBI, prosecuting attorney Irving Saypol, Judge Irving R. Kaufman, U.S. Attorney General Herbert Brownell, Supreme Court Chief Justice Fred Vinson and President Eisenhower.

In contrast, Joseph H. Sharlitt, in his book *Fatal Error* revealed these schemes with legal and ethical clarity. Although my case was very different from theirs, the Rosenbergs' aspirations for world peace made me feel solidarity with them.

My telepathic conversations – primarily with my family, but also with Leslie and Vladimir – were my "break-outs" from prison. Through them, I kept informed on local, national and global struggles for justice. Although protest was often ignored or downplayed in the major media, I kept faith that people would eventually wake up. Creation was good and redemption promised, even though the dark side now seemed to reign. Revolution awaited the consciousness that history would provide. God was still in charge.

I thought about the different understandings of God. There were those in power who talked about God, but their understanding of God was very different from mine. I wondered what God meant to some of my fellow prisoners. I had learned from Gracie that there was actually a Certificate of Ministry program right here in Sing Sing. Gracie had read about it in *Sojourners Magazine*. The program had been founded by Dr. George Webber of New York Theological Seminary. Several inmates had earned Master of Theology degrees, and some, upon release, had taken on responsible positions, bringing hope to communities plagued with poverty, drugs and violence.

Theology "in the house." Prison ministries expressing different faiths were not uncommon, but an actual degree program was remarkable. Solid academic training could make a real difference. With prisons increasingly focused on punishment over rehabilitation, I wondered what pressures had been put on the New York System to allow this left-leaning program. Yet, here it was – in the same Sing Sing which had electrocuted more than six hundred men and women during the 1930's, 40's and 50's.

Regarding my thoughts on this, I could only reflect on what I was told, because I had no contact with other prisoners. I thought a lot about what else might be happening with the prisoners. Particularly, I wondered how the agendas of the prison industrial complex – slave labor for private corporations – had impacted Sing Sing. As a federal prisoner (like the Rosenberg's) I was isolated from those convicted of more conventional crime. Among them, no doubt, there were the wrongly convicted, as well as the guilty, and among the guilty, some whose sentences were unfairly long. Some of them, as well as the rehabilitated and repentant, welcomed such a program. The studies empowered them and those they served.

In the enlightened atmosphere of our small church, Gracie and I had appreciated how modern scholarship could liberate the Bible from Christendom. Bad theology had fostered oppression, but intelligent understanding could reveal scripture as a tool for liberation.

My ministry was painting and drawing. My best work was spiritually inspired, sometimes with Biblical reference. Liberation theology, whatever the media, was one way to break through the false consciousness that bred poverty and violence.

Unfortunately, many progressives, both religious and secular, fail to see how the needs of finance capital inevitably lead to exploitation and war. I believed that those who sought only reform were complicit in the worsening danger. I believed that all who understood the necessity for economic justice (those of various faiths and the non-religious) must join in solidarity to confront, struggle against and overcome the reign of capital.

In prison, I felt powerless. I desperately wanted to be actively participating in the struggle. For several minutes, I paced my cell. Then suddenly, I was startled by a flash of light, up near the ceiling and just a few steps ahead. As it moved slowly toward me, the flashing ceased. It was my long-awaited little Orb!

Finally! I stood still, hoping for a message that my liberation would come soon. But that is not what I heard. Instead, I learned that Sing Sing would continue to be my "residence" for a few more months. But now there was a definite time for my release and enhanced compensations for my remaining incarceration. My release would come just before the millennium, about seven months from now. And until then, through a process of dematerialization and materialization, I would be spending time at home, undetected by prison authorities. My dematerialization/materialization would be like those in the science fiction series, "Star Trek."

Now, under the management of the "force," this fiction would become my reality. The idea was exciting, but also a little scary. Although I already believed in the scientific and spiritual possibility, I wondered if there was a possibility of malfunction. What if it only worked partially, leaving me in the wrong place at the wrong time? The little Orb needed to remind me that my rescue was critical to their plan; they could not let me down.

But I did have another worry. If a crisis situation were to erupt at Sing Sing, there could be an unexpected cell check. The replica of me "sleeping" in my cell while I was home would not be adequate for a prison full alert. The little Orb would need to get me back instantly. The real me would have to be present and accounted for.

In the next few months, I "went home" about once a week. The visits were, of course, strictly private, with only Gracie, Sarah, and occasionally Leslie present. Obviously, I could never be seen by anyone else until I was fully liberated. I fantasized what the shock and confusion of my Westbeth neighbors might be if they could see me walking around our hallways. Such amusing thoughts helped Gracie and I bear the tension of these unearthly, but welcome, experiences. Sarah enjoyed not only my presence, but the phenomenon itself. Leslie stayed cool.

Of course, an important part of my visits was the private time I had with Gracie. The consummation of our relationship at these times was unlike any we had ever known before. The bond derived from these intimate trysts gave us new strength, which remained with us even when we were apart. Plus, with the little Orb's assistance, we were able to see each other telesthetically from my cell. We were thankful for these privileges.

There was extra pleasure for Sarah when I was home on special nights – the eve of Father's Day, and soon after, my birthday. I was even allowed to watch fireworks with my family on the Fourth of July, although, as victims of the political system, our celebration was not patriotic.

In light of more recent history, the site for our viewing was particularly strange. Through dematerialization/materialization (d/m), all of us, including Leslie, found ourselves at the very top of the World Trade Center, above the observation deck, completely alone and out of sight. There we enjoyed a spectacular view of Macy's fireworks set off from the East River – and more displays westward, lighting the New Jersey skies. The rhythmic explosions of color were a pyrotechnic masterpiece.

We chose to make this a celebration of hope for a liberated world – a hope for God's Kingdom. By thus liberating the intended symbols, we envisioned the fulfillment of the Biblical promise of creation – a "good" world of impartial justice, equally shared resources and everlasting peace. At the same time, I was painfully aware of the contradictions.

The time held special significance of another kind. On July 3, hundreds of protesters, some of whom braved arrest for civil disobedience, had demonstrated in Philadelphia at the Liberty Bell and in San Francisco's Union Square, demanding freedom for Mumia Abu-Jamal, Leonard Peltier, and other political prisoners, including me. The protests continued through the Fourth, with temperatures here approaching 100 – the heat of summer and the heat of rising anger.

Sadly, not all of the anger was focused in meaningful protest. Too many were hurting themselves or their brothers and sisters. Too many groped about in the darkness of false consciousness, complicit in their own oppression. It would truly be a miracle when the blind could see.

Chapter 22

ON THE AIR

To make the blind see. Considering all that had taken place since our first sighting of the UFO, miracles did not seem so far fetched. But changing consciousness would be a different kind of miracle. The "force" was working to bring this about, but it needed me, and it needed Vladimir, not only to co-operate with their plan, but to go beyond our already established creative communications. I desperately wanted to contribute whatever I could, but I wondered what I should be doing. My being in prison did inspire some to organize, but I felt a need for a more active role. In prison, I was denied tools for creative expression.

Mumia, still in prison in Pennsylvania, was allowed to write columns for the alternative press. As much as our oppressors feared and hated this award-winning militant Black journalist, they could not completely restrict his Constitutional right to free speech. The authorities claimed, however, that my alleged crime of espionage required more restrictive measures. When Leslie's attempts to challenge this were denied, our first thought was to initiate public protest, but we feared a backlash against those political prisoners who were still allowed to speak out.

But the prankish "force" had another plan – a plan that would fulfill my need to again communicate with the WBAI audience and beyond. This was the plan: I would fall into the same dream-like state that I experienced when the little Orb led me through the interior of the top-secret military building. And, just as then, seeing but unseen, I would go spirit-like with the little Orb, this time into the warden's office, where he would be sleeping in his easy-chair, as was his after-lunch habit. Routinely, he protected his rest period by having all incoming calls relayed to his deputy's extension, leaving his phone free for my use. By telepathic thought, I could connect the phone with any number I chose. My choice was the alternative radio station, WBAI.

"Hello, 'BAI. You're on the air." It was talk show host, Bernard White. Thanks to my extra-terrestrial friends, I was speaking and listening telepathically through a phone untouched by me.

"Hello, Bernard."

"Hello. Who's calling?"

"It's Mark DeLouise calling from Sing Sing."

"Mark DeLouise calling from Sing Sing?"

Bernard had actually been expecting my call. Although he could not know all of the events that had lead up to this phone call, he knew that the now famous Mark DeLouise had had to be involved in something beyond normal experience. It was because of this awareness and because of Bernard's revolutionary consciousness that he had been chosen to receive my call. Although not totally convinced that it was really me, he was not about to miss this opportunity to bring me to his audience.

I began with a statement of appreciation,

"Bernard, first off, I want to thank 'BAI listeners who are following my case, believe in my innocence, and are giving me their support."

With my statement of gratitude, Bernard's astute questions and comments, and my hopefully informative answers, we were heard for about fifteen consciousness-raising minutes before my time was up. The warden continued to snooze, as the little Orb and I exited his office, as invisibly and silently as we had entered it.

Gracie, Sarah and Leslie knew of this plan and would have

been listening. Back in my cell, I contacted them, so that we could share in our excitement. Late that night, my d/m visit home was an opportunity to learn more about the impact on my radio audience. After I had ended contact with Bernard, call after call had come in from listeners. There were, of course, many unanswerable questions and many comments – most, according to Gracie, positive. Some had their doubts that it was really me, and others refused to even consider that it might be me, while still others (among them persons who actually knew me), believed that this was much too serious to be a hoax.

The New York Times, not unexpectedly, reported it as a probable hoax; perhaps perpetrated by people in my support group, using an assigned imposter.

The next day and again the next, I repeated my trips to the warden's office. One day I called the governor's number; the next day, the president's. I hadn't expected to speak to either; my point was just to identify myself to the aide who answered the phone, so that my calls would be reported and registered as having come from the warden's office.

When the calls did show up as made from the warden's office, Warden Philip Gates went wild. From the timing, he knew that the calls had been made during his nap time, but he could not see how anyone could have entered his office. He ordered an immediate investigation and a tightening of surveillance. There were no more afternoon naps.

A leak to the press started the story spreading like wildfire. "The man is locked up tight," Gates told reporters. "This all is simply impossible."

The story was now out in newspapers and on television, all over the world. Lenno, Letterman and the rest of the late night comics tried to outdo each other, mocking the prison's embarrassing incompetence. It was interesting publicity for me, but I felt anxious about unknown consequences.

The FBI came to check for my fingerprints on the warden's phone. Clearly, my voice was the same as that on the subpoenaed tape of my

WBAI interview. The telephone records ruled out the hoax/imposter theory. What was anyone to think?

The investigation was effectively stalemated and the public confused. It was a grave embarrassment. Soon the story was quietly withdrawn from the major media. All seemed ominously quiet. Perhaps a lull before the storm? At first we were anxious, but then I reminded myself, and reminded Gracie and Leslie as well, that the "force" was still in charge. My telepathic communication with those I loved and trusted helped us keep things in perspective.

Soon the little Orb gave me new instructions. Following the model of the data collection for Leona Fischer's bathroom, I now was guided on an invisible walk through the prison. Ironically, at the same time, the warden also was walking through the prison, and, although guards stood outside his door, there was no one in his office. Along my way, I carefully noted certain details; then ended my tour in the office. There I was instructed to note the exact location of significant items on the desk and on the walls, and the precise arrangement of the furniture, a task which was in no way impeded by the increased surveillance. Telepathically, using the warden's telephone as before, I called Amy Goodman's "Democracy Now" segment on WBAI, to give her and her listeners a fully detailed account of my Sing Sing tour, while I was presumedly locked down in solitary confinement. I fantasized a hysterical response from the establishment press.

I was wrong. Even the more progressive media barely mentioned the story. It was, after all, so incredible, that few dared to appear to take it seriously. Yet, a flurry of internet reports sparked countercultural debate. Gradually arguments for and against believing my account began to permeate varied forms and locations of discourse. Here, and around the world, people were beginning to question "common sense."

Could such shaking of established perception lead to more important questions of "reality?" Could such a debate help shift consciousness? Here, no matter how the establishment chose to respond, there would be debate. Eventually, in spite of the incredulous nature of my report, the story would be told, because it would sell newspapers and magazines. The prison authorities did not want the story out, but they could not stop it for long.

When the story did come out, the establishment did its best to promote disbelief. In sensationalized versions, it was used to distract people from the destructive role that the U.S. government was playing. For example, how many Americans knew how their tax dollars were being used to favor greed over need, globally and here at home?

What would it take to wake people up? Oppression had fueled revolutions in the past, but real change would require vision.

Chapter 23

VLADIMIR RE-CONNECTS

Gracie had told me about a story in the *New York Times*, based on information from the Russian press: In the prison where Vladimir was held, official papers from the administrator's office had been found in the kitchen, while an assortment of small kitchen utensils appeared on the prison administrator's desk. The kitchen worker who had found the papers also learned that his missing kitchen utensils had been found in the administrator's office. Of course, prison officials did not want this incident public. But before they could make this clear, the excited worker had already told the press.

Based on my experience of spirit-like prison travel, I assumed that Vladimir, with the help of the little Orb, was responsible for this mysterious switch. There was no problem beyond the re-arrangement of prison articles, but this was quite enough to upset prison authorities. They, of course, could make no more sense of this than their American counterparts could make of my inexplicable ventures. Once the story was out in a Moscow paper, it was, of course, denied completely. But it had already become world news.

I wondered what Vladimir would tell me about the incident. It had been several weeks since we had been in touch. But before I could initiate telepathy, I heard his voice.

"Mark, I heard that you were on the radio. We need to talk."

"Vladimir, I was just going to contact you. How are you?"

"I'm doing well, under the circumstances. The "force" is looking out for me. It couldn't get me on the radio, but it helped me make a stir."

"I heard. We are both up to mischief. The little Orb is helping us to tell the world it doesn't know what it's dealing with. The ruling powers must be in a quandary."

Vladimir went on to say that the prison authorities had ordered the press to drop all mention of the incident. He and his family, with whom he shared the same communication and visiting privileges that I enjoyed, continued to find the incident most amusing. His wife Galima told him of my radio interviews, which had been reported in the Moscow press, before that story also was suppressed. His family was holding strong, and prison life was better.

"My high profile status has motivated the prison to ease up on the grueling treatment," he explained. "It doesn't want bad publicity. Prison life is hard, but it's not the Gulag."

We discussed what might happen next. With the Cold War ended, the Soviet Union dismantled, and Russians eating under the golden arches of McDonald's, there was a different wariness between the nations. Organized crime played an important role in both nations, but was more open in Russia. On one level Russia was our client state; on another, our competitor; and perhaps, on still another, a latent power, waiting to find the right allies. The spy thing brought out more awareness of the oppositional forces. Now, caught up in this perplexing exigency, could Russia see fit to ally itself with the U.S. to search for an explanation? Such an alliance could be face-saving, even if other tensions remained. The nations could choose to announce some joint official investigation, or agree to share independent investigations. But if they learned nothing from either Vladimir or me, how could they find answers?

There was, in fact, no way that they could explain this bizarre sequence of events until the "force" was ready to reveal itself. Even

Vladimir and I could not know the final outcome, although we both believed that it was necessary and good.

"There will finally be real peace," said Vladimir.

"I believe that," I said. "Peace with justice."

This story that I share with you, dear reader, climaxes at the millennium. As 21st century readers, you are all too painfully aware of how far we are from this anticipated vision. Perhaps you do not believe it can ever be fulfilled. I, however, must share my belief with you, because otherwise what would be the point of our existence? For centuries, a few among us have struggled against the tide, but the tide has yet to turn. Can what is now counterculture ever become mainstream, or will there need to be outside intervention? None of us have the answer, but I hope that we can be open to possibilities.

I return now to the story as pre-millennial Mark. In this time, Gracie and I try to imagine what the "force" has promised. We try to fantasize how it will motivate people to work together. Such an event should turn things around. Vladimir shares my dream,

"Galima and I have discussed this many times. During the time of the Soviet Union, we hoped for real communism – a world of sharing and co-operation. Our hope has not died."

There were several more concrete things that we shared as well. We were, as you already know, both painters and social activists and fathers who were close in age. Now I learned that Galima was Sino-Russian, meaning that we were both inter-racially married. I offered a suggestion,

"Our families need to meet. When we are both free, we can all spend time together."

"Of course," Vladimir responded. "It will be a challenge without the little Orb to give us a common language, but we'll make out."

"Maybe I should start working on my Russian now."

"And I on English. I do know a few words. Galima knows a few more, and Natasha has been learning some in school. Natasha and Nikolai want to go up on the Empire State Building, where the original King Kong climbed."

We laughed about the universal popularity of King Kong. The

first movie version was still the classic, even halfway around the world. Its symbolism made a mockery of racism.

Then I told Vladimir about my long held wish to see the colorful steeples and domes of St. Basil's Cathedral. Vladimir explained that Tsar Ivan the Terrible ordered the cathedral built in 1554, to celebrate his final victory over the Tartars in Kazan. We then impressed each other with knowledge of each other's national history. Vladimir knew more about America's Civil War and our civil rights movement than most U.S. citizens did. I was able to discuss the October Revolution, the roles of Lenin and Trotsky, and the betrayal of Stalin.

But before I could make any serious reference to Russian/Soviet history, I heard a telepathic signal from Gracie. I explained the interruption to Vladimir and said "good-bye" for now, but we would speak again. He and I were finally developing a bond.

Chapter 24

THE YOUNG SCHOLAR

"Mark, I finally reached you. Are you o.k.?"
"I'm fine. I have been talking with Vladimir. I just realized that you were trying to reach me. What's up?"

"A defense alert for Mumia. Ron Hill just signed a new warrant for him to be executed December 2. Protests are being organized. We will stop it!"

The date was about seven weeks away. Hill signed it October 13, just nine days after the Supreme Court rejected Mumia's request for a constitutional review of his conviction. The protests would be in several cities, nationally and internationally. Gracie and Sarah would be joining the one in Philadelphia. I reminded Gracie that all my love and prayers would be with them.

"No justice, no peace!" The staccato-like commands of the chant leader would be understood and misunderstood. Their serious meaning would be beyond the consciousness of many. I imagined myself as one of the speakers trying to lay ground for insight.

I would try to help the protesters see, as I have come to see, that we are involved in a cataclysmic showdown between the spiritual forces which influence our will to express what is good and/or what is evil in our human nature. To succeed in our struggle, that realization is crucial.

Buoyed by my militant thoughts, my strong sense of alliance with the "force," and my abiding faith that the course my life had taken was in keeping with God's will, I became completely relaxed, closed my eyes and soon was sound asleep. I awoke with a shock to find myself at home in our bed, and Gracie greeting me with a smile. I guess I was sleeping so soundly when it was time for my d/m trip that the little Orb did not want to disturb me, but told Gracie how to expect me. I gratefully hugged her, and then asked for Sarah.

Sarah had been doing her homework. When she heard my voice, she shouted "Dadeee!" and headed in my direction.

There were more hugs and lots of questions. I told them about my conversation with Vladimir, and they shared with me their plans for the Philadelphia trip.

Being home with Gracie and Sarah was always a power charge for my often waning spirit. Knowing that they were in the struggle lifted my spirit. Afterwards, Sarah would be sharing her experience with her classmates.

When the day of the protest came, I did indeed get telepathic reports, both from Sarah and Gracie. The promised pictures were saved for my next materialization visit, as Leslie feared that they might create a problem for me if mailed to the prison. After the protest, Mumia's attorneys, who had filed a petition for Habeas Corpus Relief, won a stay of his execution. The federal judge signed the stay order on October 26. Because we believed that the protest may have helped Mumia's attorneys, Sarah felt that it had been important to be part of it. She was grateful that her dad was protected by the "force" and hoped that Mumia would be protected, too.

Sarah's growing interest in Mumia led her to voracious reading on his case. She learned from books, videos and articles, and kept a journal of case developments, public responses and her own observation, to use for an essay in his defense. She even became an organizer, explaining Mumia's case to her friends and recruiting them to help in the distribution of leaflets.

November came. Sarah gathered more information for her Mumia essay. On November 6, she and Gracie went to the Workers

World Party Conference. Hundreds were in attendance, but few her age. She was excited by some of the speeches from party leaders, including the party's presidential and vice-presidential candidates, Monica Moorehead and Gloria LaRiva.

Later, Sarah visited New York University's Law School, to hear a panel discuss the gross miscarriage of justice in Mumia's case, which the attorneys hoped could be the basis for an evidentiary hearing and a new trial. Here, she was the only child among many adults, most of whom were law students, faculty or practicing lawyers.

"And there she sat," Gracie had reported, "in rapt attention, taking notes, trying to fathom the legal language. 'Leslie,' she said, 'you're a lawyer. What's a *habius carpus*, and how do you spell it?'"

Gracie went on to say that Leslie had cheerfully and patiently obliged her with the correct spelling and meaning. People sitting near her were quite amazed by her interest. And when they overheard her recognition of Robert Meeropol, son of the Rosenbergs, they must have wondered who this child might be.

It was now mid November. Our friend Marie from the International Action Center had called Gracie to ask if she and Sarah could travel to Plymouth for the Native American Day of Mourning. They might have gone, but Thanksgiving was a night for my next dematerialization/materialization visit. Gracie just said that it was a hard time for them to make the trip, but that they would be with them in spirit. Gracie would use the day to teach Sarah the facts of this history that were not being taught in school.

Sarah would learn how Captain Miles Standish led his men against the natives in 1622. She would learn that the severed head of the victims' leader was publicly displayed as a warning to other native people of more to come. Much more did come in 1636 when hundreds from the Pequot nation were massacred and their land, now Rhode Island and southern Connecticut, taken.

Sarah already knew some of the history of genocidal wars against America's native peoples, and how they had been banished from their lands. Now she would learn that political prisoner, Leonard Peltier, a warrior of the American Indian Movement (AIM) was sentenced to two consecutive life terms in federal prison for the killing of two FBI agents, in spite of the FBI's own admission that their killer is unknown. The violence occurred at a government shoot-out on the Pine Ridge Reservation in 1975.

As Gracie told me about the history lessons, I thought about Sarah's learning style. Sorting and reflecting would come before any questions. She would note information in her journal, perhaps to be used later in an essay. Then when she was ready to ask them, the first questions would be for confirmation of answers already fully or partly figured out; finally her what-else-is-there-to-know questions would come. Already, Sarah was a scholar. My imminent visit home would be especially rich.

Chapter 25

* ———————— *

GETTING SMARTER

My Thanksgiving visit brought me in touch with my much matured daughter. Not only was she a source of pride, but also an inspiration to resource more of my own thinking skills. As a painter, I had always worked to complement creativity with structure, but I had never before been so challenged, both personally and historically, to make sense of my world. Earthly powers were leading us toward disaster. I needed to do my own sorting and reflecting to understand how things might change. I had many questions.

Currently I was hearing of the Seattle protest against the World Trade Organization. Tens of thousands of people had gathered to peacefully protest the WTO. Not surprisingly, they were assaulted with tear gas, pepper spray, rubber and plastic bullets and "flash and bang" concussion grenades. The action was soon dubbed, "The Battle of Seattle." Many were beaten and arrested.

Among the protesters was a large union presence, including social service employees and steel workers. The International Long Shore and Warehouse Union closed down the west coast docks, while some of the local residents, angered by the police violence, joined them. They did shut down the conference.

Yet, as I write this story today, I know how our history has evolved without the intervention of the "force." Labor continues to lose strength and many who oppose today's poverty and violence have lost faith in protest. Still, the WTO protest and the many significant actions since are signs that the world has its own potential for salvation. The struggle between good and evil continues. Even if there could actually be an extraterrestrial intervention, justice could not be magically won. The "force" can only provide a wake-up call. Prophets and, in my tradition the Messiah, have been sending out calls for centuries, but messages have been distorted and misunderstood. Would the "force" be more clear and convincing?

Of course I had more personal concerns, but they could not be separated from the larger reality. And, in that I understood my personal suffering to be serving the greater good, I continued to feel a sense of privilege. Something big was around the millennial corner.

December brought me and the world closer to that corner. Because our "information age" was computer dependent, Y2K, the unprogrammed year, became a matter of concern, in spite of assurances that the necessary adjustments were being made. Meanwhile certain fundamentalist Christians predicted that this would be the end time.

But millennial concerns in no way curbed the usual frenzy of holiday shopping. Consumption in America hit record levels, even as a majority of the world's peoples lived in poverty. Our "Babylon" was allowed to build on violence and oppression, while millions still clung to their faith in the "American dream."

Many, who had awakened to the contradictions, understood the importance of solidarity with oppressed peoples at home and around the world. A few understood their responsibility to "educate, organize and agitate." Most, however, chose to sleep. No amount of clamor in the streets seemed compelling enough to wake them. I could not be out in the streets now, but I understood that I was playing a crucial role.

As I counted the departing December days, the little Orb kept me informed of news events. My home visits, even my telepathic and telesthesian contacts were now limited and the mass media could not be trusted, so this communication was especially appreciated.

Restrictions on my home contacts related to the increasing

electromagnetism around our planet. The "force" was receiving electrical impulses warning of the possibility of imminent detection by earth-monitored satellites. The "force," therefore, sometimes had to shut down communication circuitry in order to avoid such detection. Because, however, I so desperately wanted to connect with my family, I questioned these restrictions. With my feelings of isolation and resentment, even with the little Orb's explanation, I at first refused to understand. But then I reminded myself of Sarah's logical approach to problem solving. I should, at the very least, be as conscientious as my ten year old in my thinking. I came to understand that the restriction on my family contacts was necessary.

As I resourced my own capacity for rational thinking, I came up with a theory. Knowing the warring nature of earth's imperialists, the extraterrestrials knew the danger of being discovered within air combat range. Such an exposure could have led to a disastrous military confrontation – an aborted "force" mission and a devastated USA, along with its shepherded imperialist allies. Anticipating the possibility of such a threat, the "force" could not yet allow itself to be revealed. There could be no interception of its communications. This evasive tactic was safer than any attempt at blocking or redirecting the search impulses of earth's satellites or their radar systems of tracking stations. Such blocking or redirecting could have marked their alien presence.

I felt good about being able to formulate my theory. With some effort, I was actually thinking smarter. It gave me new confidence, as I anticipated an expanded relationship with the extraterrestrials. My theory was confirmed by the little Orb, who began to show me increased respect. It seemed like we were becoming friends. I wondered if Vladimir was having experiences similar to mine and if he had shared his insights with his little Orb which moved them towards some sort of similar friendship.

Friendship with extraterrestrials! Soon the importance of that relationship might be acknowledged by the world. What a leap that would be from our dishonor as convicted spies! Vladimir and I might turn out to be heroes. In spite of the tension I was feeling in having to take instructions from the "force," I was beginning to feel my own power. Perhaps the same was true for Vladimir.

A visit from the little Orb brought me out of my imaginings. Because my little informant was in my cell with me, it could simulcast news from countercultural radio without the risk of interception. I was thus brought up to date. In addition, the little Orb confirmed my speculations relating to Vladimir – that his experiences were parallel to mine. My little Orb seemed to imply that this was something I should not have to question: Vladimir was my counterpart. My question had been a waste of mental energy. I would need to learn economy of thought and action, an energy conservation imperative when stakes are high. Such mental process was basic to the modus operandi of space travelers and something I too needed to acquire. I was embarrassed by not already knowing this, but enriched by the knowledge itself.

Chapter 26

"BEFORE THE MILLENNIUM"

Vladimir and I had been promised our liberation "before the millennium." We did not know exactly what "before" meant, but, for me, the holidays were an excuse to avoid the question. The little Orb apparently saw no reason yet to encourage my speculation. Its communication stayed in sync with my adaptations to prison life and my now accustomed privileges.

"It is possible, Mark, that the way may be clear for you to be with your family Christmas Eve."

Even though it was not a guarantee, the little Orb's message raised my spirit. It demonstrated a continuing effort to attend to my personal needs, even though I was part of a much larger plan. The "force" would do what it could to bring me together with my family for holiday time. If their team could plot the electromagnetic spectrum safely, I would be afforded a trip home. It was now December 20. If all went well, I would have my visit in four more days.

The holidays made me think of my parents. My incarceration was hard on them. Actually they were already on my mind because of current news relating to their native land, Panama. Just a few days before, December 15, the Canal and former U.S. military bases there were turned over to the government of Panama. My father had worked on the Canal before I was born; then left for New York to prepare the way for his family. Soon I was to arrive in New York as a six-month-old immigrant in my mother's arms, along with three older sisters and my older brother. Since that time, the U.S. continued to dominate the region. Today, December 20, was the tenth anniversary of the 1989 U.S. invasion of Panama, allegedly in pursuit of its war on drugs, but in reality to affirm its control. Many Panamanians were killed and their property destroyed. Although I had never been back to the area, I identified with its people. I knew that, in spite of the Canal now "belonging" to Panama, if there was any challenge to American dominance, violence could occur again. The United States would do whatever it determined necessary to serve the needs of its capital investors. The anger that I already felt toward American imperialism was deepened by my personal connection.

The next few days seemed to drag. I meditated and sketched. As I read ancient scriptures, I reflected on how imperialism had changed; how technology had brought oppression and violence closer to apocalypse. On the 23rd, the little Orb reported that it looked as if the "force" would be able to avoid detection by Earth's observers, but there was no certainty.

The hour was late, and I needed sleep But I tossed and turned, as my tension refused to subside. I met the day, bleary-eyed, wondering, weary and tense. I had blamed my anxiety on the uncertainty of my Christmas visit, but knew that my real concern went much deeper. As much as I longed for my soon-to-arrive freedom, I worried about what this freedom would require.

All that I could do now was wait. No longer insistent on my own gratifications, I tried to think more clearly about life after prison. Because we could not understand the extraterrestrial plan, my family and I had been dependent on the "force." Soon more would be revealed to us, so we would have to be responsible for more of our own decisions. Those decisions would be informed by events that would change mass consciousness, and bring a new awareness of our place in the universe.

Within the prison, there were now special religious services for the holidays. But even if I were not in solitary, I could have no interest in them. Their purpose was to pacify, not to awaken. Alone, I prayed and asked God to strengthen me for the challenges ahead.

Just then there was a familiar bright flash. The little Orb was hovering over my head. I awaited its communication, until at last it announced cheerily,

"Mark DeLouise, you are going home Christmas Eve!"

I had been so focused on my anticipated responsibilities that I had almost forgotten about this gratification. But this Christmas Eve visit was not just for me, but for Gracie and Sarah as well. My heart filled with joy as I looked forward to our sharing this time together. The little Orb would give my family this news, also.

Late Christmas Eve, I materialized in my home and was greeted with warm hugs and then what had become our traditional Christmas Eve supper – pasta with calamari. Although much of our time was simply focused on sharing our thoughts and feelings, we did decorate a small tree. Sarah played some holiday CD's. My favorite was *Go Tell It on the Mountain*, because it proclaimed a liberating savior. Since most holiday music was overly sentimental, I asked Sarah to play *The International*, which celebrated the Paris Commune. We talked about how the struggle for justice and peace related both to the Paris Commune of 1871 and to the ministry of Jesus. It seemed to me that the workers of the commune understood the biblical imperative for justice and peace better than most within the faith, so for us the communist classic had a spiritual meaning. We had all sung it at socialist rallies, but it was important to sing it now:

Arise, you prisoners of starvation. Arise, you wretched of the earth;

For justice thunders condemnation – a better world's in birth. No more tradition's chains shall bind us. Arise, you slaves no more in thrall.

The earth shall rise on new foundations. We have been naught;
    we shall be all!

'Tis the final conflict. Let each stand in their place.
The International Party shall be the human race!

The dream of the ancient prophets, the dream of the revolutionaries of Paris seemed to be on the edge of fulfillment. Would there be a "final conflict"? As the CD played, the three of us joined in with our "live" chorus. There we stood, facing each other in a joyful triad – fervent, but keeping our vocal volume down so the neighbors would not hear me, as they, of course, were sure that I remained in prison.

Although the chorus climaxed our celebration, there were still a few minutes left to share more intimate thoughts and feelings. Tears rolled down our smiling faces as we shared our love and anticipated my promised liberation. Then I returned to prison for morning cell check.

On Christmas day, I was offered a break from solitary, but chose to stay in my cell, wondering just how things would play out. I was rehearsed neither in word or action for the coming drama. As I waited for the curtain to be raised on the intra-galactic performance, I could only wonder what cues might be given from my extraterrestrial director. Soon the whole world would know about the "force."

My anxiety returned. Perhaps in response to this, I had what can only be explained as a paranormal experience. Suddenly I found myself in a fetal position within a transparent womb-like bubble, rising to the ceiling of my cell. Strangely, I was not alarmed, but rather I felt comforted and protected. Then a voice said,

"Be not afraid. All will be well with you and your family."

This was not the voice of the "force." Rather, it seemed to be some sort of spirit, bringing a gift of rebirth. The experience could not have lasted more than a minute, because soon I was back on my prison cot.

Later, I contacted Vladimir. Vladimir had had the same experience, as startling for him as it had been for me. Although he identified himself as an atheist, he was a very spiritual person.

We explored our feelings on spirituality, as human beings and as artists, and asked ourselves many questions. We understood that the experience had to be connected to our anticipated liberation.

We were not sure when our liberation would come. Would it be the very eve of the new millennium, Friday, December 31? With this time soon approaching, we shared our hopes and concerns. Soon we would no longer be able to contact each other; nor would we be able to visit our families.

Numinous fantasies floated in my mind. They began with a flashback to the time when Gracie and I, in rapt astonishment, first saw the UFO masquerade as star, then suddenly streak across the sky. Flashes of my other strange experiences sped by in virtual reality sequence.

Vladimir and I were caught in an incredible collaborative effort with our galactic neighbors. In order to get from their "there" to our "here," these extraterrestrials needed something far beyond our technology. I believed that they could not have accomplished this without the spiritual dimension.

Without sleep, I met the final dawn of the twentieth century. It was December 31, 1999. I still did not understand what special responsibilities awaited me, but the image of my bubble encapsulation calmed my thoughts. I was anxious and super sensitive to sounds outside my cell, yet full of joy because at last I would be leaving this dreary prison, fully vindicated. Whatever demands would soon be made on me, I felt empowered to summon my strength.

As I waited, I reminisced. I remembered my first encounter with Agent Burns. Then I thought of his lovely wife Jenny, with whom we had lost contact. We really liked Jenny, but realized how impossible a reconnection with her would be, as long as she was Mrs. Burns.

Thinking of them brought burdensome images of the other government agents and their associates – Colonel Bill Carrington and May and the attractive Tina Watson, who had visited me at Westbeth with the devious Tim Bennett. Had I not had someone like Gracie to hold me, Tina might have been a serious temptation.

My attention was drawn back to the guards patrolling the corridor.

Fragments of their conversation focused on the passing century. They took pride in the ascendance of the American state as undisputed super power, and looked forward to its continuing dominance, by any oppressive and/or violent means necessary. It seemed that they could not hope or imagine anything better.

My experiences, however, had taken me beyond the hopes of faith. I knew that things would be different, even as the struggle continued. This knowledge brought me a spiritual calm more powerful than my very real anxieties. I lay down to get some much needed rest. At 11:55, the little Orb awakened me. In the last few seconds of the old millennium, it counted down to the new: ten, nine, eight, seven, six, five, four, three, two ... And then there I was, standing with Gracie and Sarah on the Westbeth roof. It was January and cold, but we were warm. Overhead was a giant spaceship, apparently not yet visible to the throngs of celebrants honking horns, ringing bells, banging pots and pans, and shouting, "Happy Twenty-first Century!"

They could not yet know that the world was about to be changed forever.

\

Chapter 27

* ————— ⊙ ————— *

THE ARRIVAL

For a few minutes, brilliant fireworks continued to obscure the flashing lights of the giant command ship with its accompanying armada. It was a silent, time-controlled arrival. Gracie, Sarah and I, alerted by the little Orb, were aware of it, but the attention of the crowds below us was still focused on the pyrotechnic celebration.

Suddenly, as the little Orb had predicted, the fireworks display came to a halt. The "force" was ready to reveal its presence to all. By remote control, it had shut down the barge computers operating the rockets' release. Reveling celebrants still looked expectantly skyward for more bursts of color, but what they saw instead was beyond their imagination – the alien command ship and its armada. There was a great hush, then sounds of confusion and building panic. Police, as scared as anyone else, assumed a blustery façade, pretending they were still in charge. Vehicle drivers, looking skyward, created traffic jams, which they tried to honk their way out of.

While New York City's citizens and visitors were having this strangest-ever experience and thinking this was only happening to them, the little Orb told us that armadas of UFO's had arrived at population centers all over the world. Only in New York, however, where it was midnight, did the giant command ship appear. To Earth's darkened hemisphere and to its sun-lighted side as well, the UFO's arrived with precise synchronicity. In the time zone of Vladimir and his family, it was morning.

All but the most remote areas of the world knew simultaneously that there was a visitation. Urgently, Washington confirmed common cause with nations that had just the day before been considered enemies, as well as with established allies. Seeking a multilateral plan for defense, an emergency session of the UN Security Council was called on New Year's Day and the military staff committee assembled. China counseled a wait-and-see approach, suggesting that UN forces try to learn the purpose of the visit. Considering the manner and great numbers in which the UFO's had come, a hostile response from Earth had to be ruled out. All agreed.

U.S. representatives suggested that the visitors be greeted with a welcoming conciliatory tone, but that international vigilance should be established. All ground and sea-to-air weapons, it argued, should be ready for instant action. Russia, in agreement with China, opposed taking any military stance which could be interpreted by the visitors as a threat, potentially precipitating disaster. What the Security Council members didn't know, was that their every word was heard by the "force," and whatever they decided would in no way change what was about to happen. And what did happen brought the people of Earth to attentive silence. At various regional locations, at and beyond armada sites, the powerful, articulate voices of the "force" spoke in languages each group understood,

"People of Planet Earth, as your galactic neighbors, we come to you on an urgent mission, for good purpose, and in peace. We understand your great concern, brought about by the magnitude and encompassing manner of our unexpected presence. Our visit is not designed to bring you harm, but to make certain that you hear our critical message directly in its original purity and truth, rather than risk its distortion from your media sources. Realizing that you might act out of fear of us, we have completely disarmed your military weapons."

Those who already believed in the possibility of intelligent life outside our planet, and, more importantly, in the potential for positive interaction with such life, cautiously moved toward trust. Others continued to be gripped by fear. The visitors' message continued,

"Our visit did not just begin with this appearance. We have been making visits to your planet since 1945, when we became alarmed by your self-annihilating power. More recently, in August of 1998 to be exact, we made our first contact in preparation for this encounter. We kept our ships far out of the detection range of your most advanced space surveillance, until now, when the time became ripe to reveal ourselves.

Our preparation for this required the cooperation of two of your most courageous and trustworthy citizens. Their relationship with us, although initially reluctant, became close. These persons were chosen for their wisdom and intelligence and for their ability as visual artists, a skill essential to our mission. They and their families have sacrificed and suffered greatly for us and for you.

Your beautiful planet is greatly endangered by your own destructive forces. And, if you continue to allow those who rule violently to lay claim to your wealth, you will destroy your home. The resulting effect on our galaxy would endanger us as well, so our concern is urgent. Mark DeLouise and Vladimir Ivanov, who became objects of international notoriety in their efforts to help us (and you), are the persons of whom we speak. We have now liberated them from their unjust imprisonment. They are now happily with their families."

This announcement brought a great stir from the crowds. It was a few minutes before the "force" spoke again,

"Having just heard that their prisoners are free, the guards are frantically checking the cells which held them. They will soon see that our claim is true.

"This is the starting point from which we will virtually walk you through your history on planet Earth, so that you may clearly see how you have come to stand at the brink of your own self-destruction."

Many of us on Earth had learned something from history and did see a better way, but lacked effective strategy for change. Others saw peace only in the dominance of their nation over another, saw wealth only as personal success, rather than something to be shared, saw responsibility as obedience to corrupt power. For them, the message from the "force" was hard to accept, yet, its impact was there.

How could it have come to this? For centuries, prophets had attempted to awaken their people. The struggle of the ages continued, but time was running out. For years, Vladimir and I had been among those who were trying to change history. We hoped that our paintings might raise some consciousness, but had not expected that we would be painting according to the plan of the "force."

Now, around the world, all attention was on the arrival. From New York to Tokyo, from Moscow to Johannesburg, a deep voice from above enveloped all, including those who were remote from our population centers. It prepared Earth for a long listen,

"What we are about to relate will need your time and concentration. We want your full attention, as your understanding is critical to your survival. Although we will later provide you with documents printed in all your languages, as well as taped recordings, it is important that as many of you as possible hear our message now. We do not, however, demand that you stay out in public places. When our next communication begins, we will have taken over your radios and television, and you will be able to find us online. Return to your homes, or if you have no homes or television, we can still reach you where you are, as we are doing now. Some of you, for public or private reasons, have not been able to give us your attention, although you, too, are aware of our presence. If and when you are able, you also must hear or read our message."

Most of the world, particularly those in wintry or wet weather, welcomed the opportunity to find shelter. Many chose to gather in small groups, in homes or in public places, but others chose to be with their families or even alone. Some stayed where they were. Gracie, Sarah and I were returned (through d/m) to our Westbeth apartment.

Listening attentively, and observing with all available surveillance instruments, were the agents of governments and corporations. Those who had been at the top levels of worldly power now frantically looked for clues which could lead them back to the restoration of their positions. Religious leaders, educators and journalists who had allowed themselves to be the tools of the ruling class, had to choose between grasping at lost privilege or awakening to the possibility of their own liberation. Among the masses, many saw the Domination system crumbling away. Its claims of "freedom" were being revealed as false, as the possibility of real freedom dramatically emerged.

The "force" believed that Earth's major problem was the misuse of wealth. Having studied Earth for decades, it understood that economic conflicts were often clothed as culture conflict. But now Earth's peoples must listen as brothers and sisters, with a minimum of intercultural misunderstandings. The message of the "force" would require wide popular acceptance on Earth, in preparation for choosing the right course. No longer could class aspirations determine the use of wealth, no longer could competitive cultures waste their resources and people in war. If this essential change were to come about it would be a great threat to those of privilege, who held the spoils of exploitation. The Power that came from beyond Earth demanded humility.

Determined to succeed, the "force" waited for the optimum moment for its message to be beneficially received. "Our message will begin in one hour. Be prepared to listen and record."

During the preparation hour, an excited, apprehensive humanity headed for their chosen spots to await the message. Few wanted to be alone. Most settled in with their families, friends and neighbors to listen together. Some went to nursing homes or hospitals to be with friends or relatives, to help them understand. Those without shelter huddled together. In New York, some built fires to warm themselves in junk-filled lots and unattended parks.

The "force," from its vast galactic distance, had been studying us for centuries; which is to say that their civilization must have predated us by millenniums. As they watched our greatest super power continue its build up of nuclear weapons, they feared for our planet, and for themselves. When the pre-determined hour was up, they began their message.

Chapter 28

THE MESSAGE

The first voice was melodiously feminine. I tried to imagine what the possessor of this voice might look like. Perhaps like a beautiful Earth woman? Or a strange creature, the product of Hollywood imagination. Or something never before even fantasized. My sense was that the voice belonged to someone who looked very much like us.

"People of planet Earth, you inhabit one of the most precious jewels in the universe. We visit you from our home, the planet Lios. Our galactic location makes you our closest anthropoidal neighbors. You must know that we have not traveled this great distance as mere tourists. Perhaps you fear that we have come as invaders, seeking to conquer and colonize you. Let us assure you that that is not our mission. Our purpose is not without self interest, but it is also in your interest. It is in fact critical for our mutual survival. The protection and perpetuation of our planet and its inhabitants are directly connected to the protection and perpetuation of your planet and those of you who inhabit it. We need you to continue living so that we may continue to live. For this reason, we have no choice but to come here to advise you that the only way life on Earth can continue will be through your willingness to eliminate the oppressive system which now dominates your existence and threatens to destroy your life and the life of your planet. You must learn a new way of living, aimed at justice and peace.

"Centuries ago, like you now, we had reached a point where we were foolishly approaching the brink of extinction. Fortunately, we were then visited by a much older, more experienced galactic neighbor, who had learned to combine technology and spirituality to travel from light years away in a manner impossible through technology alone. Their planet is called "Nede," and it is as far beyond Lios as we are from you. The citizens of Nede awakened our oppressed peoples to the necessity of a united front. And, through the struggle of our masses, revolution was achieved. Our planet was saved from the suicidal greed of our ruling class. Our energies and skills are now used for life, not death. We work to fulfill the promise of creation."

Then we heard another voice, also much like that of an Earth person's. It was a male voice, clear and deep,

"I see that the word "revolution" has caused quite a stir among some of you. Many of you in exploited nations have been involved in anti-imperialist struggles, while others among you fight against your neighbors. Some of you try to imitate your oppressors, while your majority struggles just to get through each day. In more powerful nations, many of you allow yourselves to be deceived by false teachings and false hopes. Some of you are caught in cycles of self destruction. "Revolution," which once was the hope, has been clouded by counter-revolution, and seems impossible. Well, it was the same with us. When our neighbors from Nede spoke of revolution, only the few who understood history remained patient. More of us saw hope only in piecemeal reforms, or in individual success. Such thinking was leading us toward destruction.

"The grumblings we hear from those few among you who are super rich (and many who aspire to be rich) are very familiar. Our visitors from Nede heard grumbling when they visited Lios, although there were a few enlightened persons in our ruling class, as there are in yours. Your Che Guevara and Fidel Castro both sprang from the ruling class, as do even a few North Americans, who have had to keep their politics less obvious. Regardless of your status, it is important to understand, that to take revolutionary action is to begin a creative process, which can be non-violent only if the great majority of you unite. Your prophet, Vladimir Lenin, for whom the artist Vladimir Ivanov was named, observed, 'The greater the level of awareness, the less the violence.' Knowing the level of awareness in his time, he considered it unrealistic to bring about any real change through nonviolence.

Your centuries of armed conflicts have not conditioned you for peaceful solutions. The propensity of your militarily strong to rule and exploit all that they choose has led to escalating violence that, if not stopped, will lead to your extinction. We cannot predict how imminent this threat may be. We see that some among you recognize the danger, but we see no evidence that you can turn things around without help. Should you be unable to save your planet, your destruction would dangerously upset our interplanetary balance. That is why, when we were at the same point in our history, Nede came to us, and that is why we now come to you. You must find what is meaningful in your religious and secular histories to guide you toward a just and peaceful world. These histories hold a reservoir of creative inspiration and spiritual empowerment which can carry you forward."

Now again the woman's voice,

"Many of you have been caught in the chauvinistic fantasy that you are the only human species in this vast universe. Many of you could not believe that there are other planets resembling yours, similarly populated, elsewhere in this galaxy and, no doubt, in other galaxies. Such chauvinism leads to a dangerous arrogance.

Your prophets have attempted to teach you the spiritual and material principles, which when finally realized, as you shall see, become one. These principles are necessary to counter arrogance. While you have been blessed with many teachers, I will remind you of two, who, if properly understood, can be a focus for your repentance. We know these two by way of our own history, as they were known to us in previous incarnations, by names appropriate to our language, and also to the people of Nede, centuries before.

It will no doubt startle most of you to learn that these two, who are oppositionally revered, are known to you as Jesus of Nazareth and Karl Marx. Unfortunately (but predictably), the teachings of these prophets have been profoundly distorted by both believers and non-believers, as they were on Lios and Nede.

We see with some amusement that we were correct in expecting that our mention of these men would cause quite a stir among you, for different reasons, of course. Some of you associate these men with destructive forces in history. But these men cannot be held responsible for destructive ideologies that have claimed their names. Marx was not to blame for the policies of Joseph Stalin, nor was Jesus to blame for the Inquisition or the Crusades.

Marx called on people to think scientifically about how to create a better world. Jesus did not live in a scientific age, but he called on people to read the signs of the times. Both challenged their religious establishments, and called for something radically new.

The choice to separate the spiritual from the material has been a fatal error. Your dominant religious establishments are corrupt. You have ignored the call for responsible living – 'from each according to his ability, to each according to his need.' Most of you cannot see the ways in which the teachings of these two men belong together. Some of you, however, are ready to consider that possibility, and a few of you even take joy in what you hear, as confirmation of your own insight. Those of you who understand give us hope that all will go well. We count on you to explain to your fellow Earthlings the urgency of our message, enabling more of you to know what is required for your salvation. Jesus and Marx are among many who have been sent to prepare the way."

As I listened to the words of these Lios representatives, I asked myself how I might be prepared to explain this critical message. Understanding the process of scripture formation had liberated me from the oppression of Christendom. I knew that economic justice was at the heart of scripture. There could be no peace without justice. The Jesus of John's Gospel had the potential to bring people to an existential level of knowing, but admittedly I myself was not yet there. Nor could I say that I understood Marx, although I appreciated the concept of a scientific view of history. As a believer, I knew that whoever helped to build God's Kingdom was God's servant, including Marx, who argued for atheism. Could I explain what was needed for our salvation? As if to read my thoughts, the woman continued,

"The apostle that you call Paul observed that, "For now we see in a mirror dimly." We all have insufficient knowledge. Even the two Earthlings with whom our relationship has been close must struggle for clarification. Vladimir cannot believe that Jesus, among whose alleged followers are a majority driven by false consciousness, could hold a key to liberation. Mark understands much less of the writings of Marx than does Vladimir, who has made an effort to share his understanding with his people. And there are other prophets and seekers of truth that those of you from other traditions have sought out for understanding. We want you to learn from us, but you must also learn from each other.

"Let me make clear that we do not see Marx as an alter-messianic figure, nor do we understand Jesus in the way that most of you who call yourselves "Christian" do. We have seen, however, that Marx came into the world with special gifts, nurtured by his personal history and the context of his culture, that enabled him to see what others could not, but also limited his understanding.

"On all planets, those who choose justice and peace can rejoice in a permanent revolution. The question is, 'How can you be part of this?' The answer to this will require your full attention, as we navigate your disparate waters in search of your port of understanding.

"You in your world, we in our world, and all other peoples in their worlds throughout the universe, were brought into being by a force beyond our 'force,' a creator force, who ordained that we be gifts of life to each other. We were endowed with the freedom to choose love, in order to be more like our creator. Although we are not the ultimate force, we have earned the name 'force' by learning (after many terrible mistakes) to respect and share responsibility for each other. If you can come to believe, as we through faith believe, that this is the purpose of your being; and if you can turn your present destructive course around toward life-fulfilling ends; it will not be solely to save yourselves, but to save Lios, Nede, and all other neighbors in our galaxy affected by your violence. Your ways now threaten to provoke nuclear holocaust, which can, in domino sequence, bring about terminal galactic chaos. The awesome responsibility of resisting this evil falls on you."

How could the world's peoples respond to this overwhelming cosmic burden?! Around the world, most were speechless. Some, who believed that their salvation depended only on their commitment to a narrow piety, responded in disbelief; they waited to be lifted up, beyond the world they had already rejected. Others felt a great sense of shame, that they had not done more to stop the exploitation and greed that had lead to poverty and violence. Still others simply felt helpless. Soon silence gave way to pained, confused and questioning murmurs. Now the man from Lios spoke again. He would finish the message,

"We understand that what you are now hearing overwhelms you. Let me remind you that our own history was plagued with failings similar to yours. The fact that we have been able to change the course of our history, qualifies us to come to you as authentic mentors.

"Your planet has been and is a tribal battleground. You have used your differences in customs, traditions and beliefs as causes for alienation rather than opportunities for learning and enrichment. By choosing enmity over friendship, your strengths became weapons of conquest, rather than gifts to strengthen all.

"Your dependence on armed warfare has led to the development of technologies capable of wiping yourselves out, while your technologies for peace are inadequate for health and welfare. You fail to plan for populations appropriate for your resources, and then rob each other and the Earth itself. Corporate giants are sustained by the power of your super-state, as they exploit weaker members of your global community. Your earth mother suffers greatly from your disrespect. She is bombarded, polluted, and continually pillaged by those among you who demand control of her. What do you imagine her fate to be if you continue to violate her? Many among your own kind have tried to warn you and lived as redemptive examples of the way. You have been given much to inspire and guide you, but your behavior through many centuries has shown your inclination for corruption. Your Mahatma Gandhi was one among many who cautioned you against sin. Specifically, he spoke of what he called 'the seven sins.'

Wealth without work,
Pleasure without conscience,
Knowledge without character,
Commerce without morality,
Science without humanity,
Worship without sacrifice, and
Politics without principle.

Gandhi confronted imperialism, religious division and systems of cast and class. His concept of *satyagraha* (force which is born of truth and love) was and is inspiring. From East and West, from people of conscious faith and atheists of good will, Gandhi formed his understandings. 'Truth,' he said, 'is God.'"

Around the globe, people were sharing their amazement at what they were hearing. Clearly, our galactic neighbors knew us well. The voice continued,

"You have not honored your prophets. You have forgotten them, or perverted their word. But we, too, had this weakness. And having overcome it in ourselves, we can now share with you our key to the prophets, which has always been with you, as it has with us. In order to understand the prophets, you must discover the knowledge within your own being. And the key to this revelation is your own creativity, that is to say, it is your gift to discover truth and express it, so that your creativity can be shared. This expression of truth is what we call 'art,' but not all that your world calls 'art' fulfills this purpose. We have chosen our comrades, Vladimir Ivanov and Mark DeLouise, to organize your education. As 'artists,' they have been working to discover and express truth. We will continue to help them even after we have left your planet. Your survival will depend on your readiness to understand and courageously take responsibility."

So this is what the "force" had been preparing us for. Could we be ready to lead in this struggle for change ? The suffering of incarceration and disgrace had prepared our hearts and minds, and we had learned to trust the "force." Art, created not to serve the market, but rather to serve truth, was said to be a "key."

There was a patient silence from the skies and a momentary hush throughout the planet, giving Earthlings time for reflection. People began to share questions with their neighbors. For me and my family, the meaning began to take shape. As an artist, "art" was something for which I strived, but did not always achieve. Art became art only in relationship. It was the responsibility of both producer and receiver, as both were necessary for the creative process. All had to call on their experience and tradition to seek truth and attempt to communicate their understanding.

But many on Earth were still in the dark.

Chapter 29

* ───────── ✦ ───────── *

THE PLAN

While all were now called upon to access their creativity, Vladimir and I were at the center of the redemption struggle. Mercifully, we were both now secluded with our families, shielded from all public contact. Thanks to the "force," our telephones did not ring, nor was there any buzz from downstairs or knock at our door.

Before the notoriety of our "force"-designed paintings of secret military installations and our subsequent arrests, neither of us was famous. Our work had been sub culturally appreciated, but brought little income. While artists who served the needs of those in power enjoyed wealth and fame, we both needed supplementary careers. Inflation in Russia since the fall of the Soviet Union had made things particularly difficult for Vladimir and his family, who had been depending more and more on Galima's income even before his arrest. As a Communist, Vladimir had hoped that his art would bring hope to the struggle for a more Marxist Soviet Union, but he was painting against the tide. It was not long before the Soviet's spiritually-bereft bureaucracy would collapse, and Russia would emerge as a neo-colony of more powerful capitalist states. Prior to our arrests, Vladimir and I had not heard of each other, and we had yet to see each other's work.

We, of course, understood that change would have to mean new power relationships and structures for sharing wealth. The focus on "art" enabled all peoples the opportunity to become part of this change, as they discovered knowledge within themselves, and shared it with others. Change in consciousness was necessary to make a revolution work. At the same time, material changes would change consciousness. It was a dynamic that had to go both ways.

Although the extra-terrestrial visit was not a shock for us, my family and I were still in a state of awe and wonderment. Sarah turned toward me with her observation,

"The people of Lios understand the importance of art. That is why they chose you."

Somewhat embarrassed, I looked at Gracie. I believed that Sarah understood the power of art, but I knew that most of the world's peoples did not. Many believed that the Soviet Union had failed because communism was "not in human nature." A look at Soviet "art," however, shows another problem. When creativity was policed, truth was lost.

"We must seek truth and share it creatively," I said. "That is the sense in which the extra-terrestrials speak. I have been blessed with certain talents and with nurturing influences, but the world has not made it easy for me."

"Now people will understand how important your paintings are," Sarah said. "Your *Number 10* was notorious, but it was not really your painting."

These notorious "force"-designed paintings, Vladimir's and mine, had threatened U.S. and Russian power. They were, as Sarah had noted, not even our creations. The truth that they revealed was the limits of state security and the lengths that the establishment would go to punish the exposure of their destructive technology. Revealing their secrets was a creative idea, meant to bring about new perception. In that sense, the paintings were indeed "art."

Beyond the arts of previous generations, we now have technologies that afford new ways of expression and new capacities for sharing. Cinema, television and the internet have radically changed our communications. But regardless of modality, creation springs from knowledge deep within, formed by the intimate and the universal.

Art makes it possible to share knowledge and emotion, and unlock perception.

I was sure that most of the world's peoples did not understand how art could be the "key" to their salvation. There were some all over the world, however, with important insights. Vladimir and I, because of our very special relationship with the "force," would try to pull the ideas of many together. If we could get a clear concept, it would be shared with all. In order to explore our own ideas, I asked Gracie and Sarah to help me brainstorm, which, of course, they were eager to do.

"Art is a key that unlocks the way we see and hear; a key to hearts and minds," I began. Then specifically addressing Sarah, I asked, "Do you remember my explaining the structural elements of painting?"

Sarah thought a moment and then responded. "Sure. Lines, planes, colors, values ..."

"Right. And composition and perspective. Let's think about colors – their relative differences, in chromatic intensity, in value ..."

The colors need to work. They need harmony and balance, just like the world's peoples."

"Ah, yes. Around the world people come in different colors. There are different cultural values and emotional intensities. Chroma is like emotion. And perspective helps us see potential."

Gracie had been listening attentively. "And what about music? Your dad and I have talked about how making music can be a model for the world working together. You know, in a large symphony orchestra, people may speak different languages. They may not even like each other, but they love music and they are fluent in it. So together they produce complex and beautiful sound."

"Yeah," Sarah responded. "You have all these different people playing different kinds of instruments, with different notes and sometimes even different rhythms, all at the same time. And they harmonize! The composition and sometimes the interpretation take creativity, but the production takes understanding, skill and working together."

Here was Sarah, still a child, articulating this so well, while the world's leaders were messing things up, and the people allowing them to do it. The world was in discord, but no one seemed able to fix it.

"We make terrible mistakes," said Gracie. "Creativity can help us solve problems, but what some people call 'art' is used to deceive. For me, it's not art if it doesn't ring true. Art should be aesthetic, truthful and relevant."

"So who is to judge?" I asked. "Not everyone sees a painting in the same way – which is o.k., because there are levels and complexities of meaning. But sometimes people just don't get it."

Gracie had to agree, and then went on to talk about literary art. "A good novel can give us insight, and poetry can be an inspiration. When Shakespeare wrote his plays, they were good enough to last for 400 years. We respond to our own time, but some truth doesn't change."

"If we are going to reach back in time," I asked, "what has had more important impact than the Bible? The Bible has been an inspiration for good, but it has also been used for evil."

Sarah went to pull a Bible off the shelf. "It's really dumb to think that this is easy to read."

"Dumb and deceptive. There is profound truth here, but it needs to be understood in the social context in which it was written. We need to understand the symbols and the history. I cannot think of a literary work that has been more misunderstood by so many people. But let me read something which should be clear enough."

I opened the Book to Isaiah 32: 6-8 and read:

... fools speak folly, and their minds plot iniquity:
to practice ungodliness, to utter error concerning the Lord,
to leave the craving of the hungry unsatisfied,
and to deprive the thirsty of drink.
The villainies of villains are evil;
they devise wicked devices to ruin the poor with lying words,
even when the plea of the needy is right.
But those who are noble plan noble things,
and by noble things they stand.

Literary art gives Isaiah spiritual force," said Gracie. "And from other cultures, east and west, in sacred and secular images, texts and music; art unveils the timeless and speaks to the present."

"It's about truth," I said.

With that, we fell into silence. I wondered what other people around the world were discussing. What ideas were emerging? Especially, I wondered what Vladimir and his family discussed.

As had often happened, the extra-terrestrials responded to my thoughts. This time, their address was to the whole Earth.

"We have been listening! We hear that many of you are still confused and that others are resistant to the urgency of our message. But a few of you are trying to understand what 'art' is. You are trying to think about how it can empower your liberation. If you have useful insights, you must share them. Together, with your varied traditions and experiences, you can come closer to the answers you seek. As you share and teach, others will become teachers. Do we have to remind you that this is a process of love?

"You should begin immediately. Beware of those who attempt to discourage you from your efforts. Stay strong and we will leave you to continue on your own. But if negative forces overwhelm your efforts for justice and peace, we will have no choice but to subject you to supervisory intervention."

Around the world, reaction to this stern proclamation was mixed. Some, who could not begin to grasp the new understanding, were reluctant to believe that other humans could teach them; they were more willing to accept supervision by the "force."

Others, long conditioned by grotesque popular images of extra-terrestrials, shuddered at the thought of more direct encounter. As expected, the president of the world's undisputed super power called on his advisors to find some way to hold on to the appearance of control, even if it was only an attempt to establish itself as the preeminent representative of all the nations.

As a family, Gracie, Sarah and I would do our part. Whatever role the "force" had planned for us, we believed we were ready.

Chapter 30

* ———— ⑤ ———— *

THE ASSEMBLY

My tie to the "force" had earned me and my family difficult responsibilities, but definite privileges as well. In the interests of the plan of the "force," I had already experienced invisibility on a few occasions. Now, along with Gracie and Sarah, we were all made invisible in order to secretly witness a closed session of government, in which the president and vice president, members of the House and Senate, the Cabinet and the Joint Chiefs of Staff were assembled in the Capital. In the spectator gallery, we were quite alone except for the secret service agents, who were unaware of our presence. Even the elite of the press corps were kept out of the session and told to stand by and wait.

The assembly solemnly gathered. In his usual easy manner, even in the face of this incredible situation, President Clinton strode toward the lectern. There was a ripple of applause. He thanked the assembly, cleared his throat, and began speaking with measured seriousness.

"The magnitude of our current circumstance is beyond what most of us can comprehend. I have, however, been in consultation with various advisors and now believe that if we make the right choices, if and only if, we have nothing to fear. Spaceships from the planet Lios have totally neutralized our military power. According to our military analysts, this is fortunate, because we would be no match for them. I have also learned that the majority of you, but not all, believe that our visitors have come to us on a mission of peace. They have come to warn us that our capacity for nuclear destruction endangers not only ourselves, but the entire galaxy.

"Because we are now the world's only super power, some of you believe that we are no longer at risk for nuclear holocaust. I once hoped that you were right. And I believed that even if such an event were to occur, it would not affect other bodies in our galaxy. Up until recently, there had been no evidence to suggest that it would. Leading astronomers now, however, tell me that there is a conflux of forces which make that a possibility. Orbital shifts, resulting from a massive nuclear conflagration could have a domino effect which could indeed threaten even a planet as distant as Lios. It is reasonable to believe, therefore, that the people of Lios seek to eliminate any risk to themselves. I for one do not fear that Lios wishes to exploit us or our resources. Rather, they need to insure that we do not destroy ourselves and possibly their world as well."

The president welcomed the break during a moderate applause; to mop the sweat from his brow, and take the drink of water he needed more to assuage his growing uneasiness than to quench his thirst. Bill Clinton had not become president to serve the world's peoples or even the American people. No one became president of the United States without selling his soul to major corporate interests. It was corporate interests that had funded Clinton's campaign, and these interests came first. The nation's strength depended on imperial wealth. The International Monetary Fund and the World Trade Organization were there to serve corporate interests, particularly those based in the United States. The way to keep peace was to make resistance impossible. Clinton had known how to win the presidency, and he knew how to keep his job.

Now the president, always tuned in for his own survival, understood that the game rules had changed. He must seriously heed extraterrestrial counsel. The maxim – to give according to one's ability and receive according to need – was now urgently imperative instead of just a dream. Only justice and care could prevent nuclear devastation. The restructuring of society would be a very difficult, but necessary, task The world's resources and the control of the means of production would no longer lay only with a privileged few. Authority would be held by those who served the people.

Clinton knew that many now assembled vehemently resisted this reality. How then should he proceed? His prepared remarks would not work. Murmuring in the hall was building. A hand shot up from Senator Brinkbane, never the president's friend. Clinton, however, was relieved. Brinkbane's foolish ranting would give him time to put his own words together.

"Yes, Senator Brinkbane."

"Mr. President, I was sittin' here wonderin' if you had forgot that this is the United States of America that you are president of. If I heard you right, and I believe I did, you are tellin' us that America, the most powerful sovereign nation on this planet, and the one that all sensible nations on this earth, sovereign or otherwise, look to for leadership should fall down on its knees and agree to do whatever these aliens who come here from wherever the hell in outer space they choose to tell us they come from, tell us to do. We don' even let other powers here tell us what to do. Not even the U.N.

"Now you were talking about our military being neutralized. Hell, if we had gone ahead and followed through with President Reagan's star wars plan early on, we could have stopped these aliens cold before they got anywhere near us. Mr. President, I know I'm not the only one here who feels this way. I got support on both sides of the aisle. God gave us this planet to run and we will continue to run it the way we see fit. So let's just tell them aliens to go on back to where they came from and leave us to carry on with our business."

Brinkbane did have support. While most, even in his own party, would not have articulated such blatant arrogance; arrogance itself, in varied styles, prevailed. The applause following his statement confirmed this. Clinton waited for the applause to end.

But as he was about to continue, there was a sound in the spectator gallery. Still in our invisibility, the silence we had managed to keep was broken by a sneeze that Sarah had been able to only half suppress. Immediately, secret service agents, guns drawn, moved in our direction. The little Orb moved quickly to divert their attention, creating the sound of rolling marbles at the opposite side of the gallery. Just as the agents were almost close enough for contact, they rushed toward the new sound. Meanwhile, down on the main platform, the president was surrounded by other secret service. No "assassins," of course, could be found. Security moved to different positions. They remained apprehensively alert.

The event was inexplicable. The already anxious assembly grew alarmed. Sensing their distress, Clinton believed that this was an opportunity for his leadership to be respected. Ignoring the immediate incident, he refocused the assembly on the consequences of arrogance.

"Had our visitors come with evil intent – to invade, conquer, colonize, and subject us to oppression beyond our imagination --- they would have had no difficulty doing so. They took us by surprise, completely surrounded our planet, and neutralized military power in all our nations, preventing hostile confrontation. They came not in the spirit of conquest, but rather with friendliness and concern for our mutual well-being, and survival as galactic neighbors. They traveled a distance that for us would have been impossible, to warn us of the danger that we pose to ourselves and to them. And although we have zealously explored outer space and sent out signals in the hope of contacting other intelligent life, it is they who have found us.

"Senator Brinkbane, I think we should consider ourselves most fortunate that things have worked out this way. If we had succeeded in developing star wars capability, and deployed its weapons against this alien force, we would no doubt have caused some damage to their armada, traveling at great speed toward us from all directions. And having done so, we would have left our planet a wide open target for devastating return assault. Consider if you will, Senator, their fire-power, their ability to neutralize our military, and their probable technology for surgical attack that could eliminate from our planet all that they might consider expendable, including those whom they considered unfriendly. Picture, if you can, our planet badly wounded, but stable within our solar system and still viable for their colonization."

It was difficult to deny the president's words. The men and women who were thought to be the fusion components of an invincible nation ordained to rule with impunity sat for a long moment in stunned silence. Then many could be observed shifting uneasily about in their seats. Others exchanged querulous glances, seeking commiseration. For those who had basked in the allusion of power, this was humiliation.

There had, indeed, been an allusion of power. Few made it into major government position without the support of serious capital. If the people awakened to this understanding, those who claimed to lead would lose their credibility. But the majority of people still slept. Clinton, however, understood power. And he understood that his loyalty could no longer be with capital. He would heed the visitors' advice and guide the world's only super power into compliance. This was now his role. This would earn him respect. He knew how to conclude his statement.

"The likelihood of tragedy resulting from a star wars encounter was confirmed by our Joint Chiefs of Staff in a briefing this morning. I know that this assessment is troubling. But we can rise above despair and bring hope to our entire world. As leader of the "free world," we must share our resources with our sister nations to workably respond to our visitors' urgent appeal. We must turn off the road to war, which can only lead to extinction. We will seek the 'key' to our liberation, so that we may open the doors to justice and peace."

Clinton did not really know what the "key" was. But he was smart enough to understand more than most. The "key" had been only vaguely defined as "art" by the "force," so that we could come to our own understanding. "Art" itself was an ambiguous word, even for me. Although Vladimir and I had been given some authority on this concept, we would need to hear from others.

The next person to speak was Congresswoman Genevieve Rivers from Georgia. As this strikingly beautiful tall black woman rose to her feet, many turned to watch her stately movement.

"Mr. President."

"Yes, Congresswoman Rivers."

"Your counsel to heed the advice of our visitors is essential. And I appreciate your commitment to seek the 'key' to liberation. I hope that you are serious in your commitment, but I have reason for concern. My concern is based not only on your record, but the records of many of my colleagues. Even now many of you use the term 'free world,' presumably in its established code, as that part of the world in which individuals are 'free' to accumulate wealth through the exploitation of labor and the exploitation of resources which should belong to all. 'Freedom' for the few has usually meant oppression for the many. As long as our government rests on the power of capital, it is corrupt, and because of its hegemonic power, it corrupts most of the world. I hope, Mr. President, that when you speak of sharing our resources with sister nations you include those nations that are striving for a different paradigm. I know, for example, your negative judgment on Cuba. You and many of your colleagues should now be ready to learn from Cuba, which you so far have labeled a 'rogue' state, since it resists your influence.

"We are the most powerful nation in history, but we must learn as well as teach. We have much to overcome. We are plagued with racism, sexism, homophobia, police brutality, an unjust justice system and failing schools. We do not provide adequate health care or housing for our citizens. We exploit developing nations through unfair trade and usurious debt collection."

Rivers paused. Her listeners waited respectfully, whatever their disparate thoughts. Clinton was well aware of his unethical record, but he had had to play the game. Winning came first, but Clinton understood that now winning meant he would have to change. Others in the assembly did not understand this, even though it was dramatically clear that we could not survive without change. The congresswoman continued,

"Our visitors spoke of Jesus and of Karl Marx. Their understanding of both of these men seems quite different from most of our understandings here. We need to reconsider their importance for our world. And we need to remember Dr. King's observation that, 'We must learn to live together as brothers [and sisters], or we will perish together as fools.'

"The evil legacy of Stalin has clouded much of our understanding of communism. But communism is not Stalinism. Communism refers only to an economic system, in which wealth is shared according to need. We have demonized a system that can provide for all. We have celebrated a system in which the few exploit the many. Marx and Jesus sought justice for all. It should be clear by now that there can be no peace under capitalism. Who has the 'key' to this understanding?"

Signaling that she was finished, Rivers took her seat. Members of the assembly focused on her in anger, appreciation, and primarily confusion. They turned to look at the president. Feeling the weight of their emotion, Clinton tried to provoke some critical thinking.

"Fellow Americans, it seems that our colleague here is declaring herself communist. With a small 'c,' of course, for we all know that she is a Democrat. But the Democratic Party (my party) is a capitalist party. Can any of us, Democrat or Republican, take her seriously?

"Before we answer that question, we have to look at where our economic system has brought us. Some of you will say that it has made us a strong nation and that many of us have been able to fulfill the American dream. I, in fact, who came from difficult economic circumstances, am now your president. Now as president, I have a responsibility for justice. I have a responsibility for peace. As leaders of this nation, all of us have responsibility. Yet we have perpetuated a system that continues to increase the polarization of rich and poor here at home and around the world. Our system cannot survive without violence. Perhaps we need to take Ms. Rivers seriously. Perhaps we need to consider fundamental change.

"Although Ms. Rivers and I have not always agreed, I appreciate her as a person of veracity, loyalty and compassion. She has been steadfast in her legislative efforts for justice and peace. She believes that our structures for distribution of wealth must change.

Our recent history has shown that capitalism and communism cannot effectively coexist. As private industry flourishes in China, and the Soviet Union has been relegated to history, many of you are convinced that 'communism doesn't work' Does capitalism then work? Can we look at the violence and poverty in our cities and around the world and say that capitalism works? Perhaps attempts at communism have failed simply because capitalism dominates. The global economy cannot be both communist and capitalist. Which system can insure world survival?"

Clinton was almost advocating communism. Most in the assembly could not believe what they were hearing. Congresswoman Rivers' position was no surprise, but for the president to take her seriously was unexpected. Still, there was scattered applause – from some who had already established themselves as progressives and others who had been awakened by the crisis. More prevalent were grumbling and confused silence.

At that moment, the little Orb appeared. It told us that we need not witness the ensuing arguments. Instead, we should leave the building for a special visit. We had no other information, but, knowing that our invisibility would protect our movement, we prepared ourselves to go. The assembly was interesting, but there would need to be much work from the people.

Chapter 31

ABOARD SHIP

We found ourselves traveling through space toward the armada; then entering what we learned to be the command ship and headquarters of the Chiefs of Intergalactic Operations. There we were ceremoniously greeted by beings whose appearances were like Earth's racial types. They were dressed in dark gray coverall uniforms, with what looked like shoe-socks on their feet, red belts at their waists, and gold quarter moons on their shoulders, the number of moons apparently denoting rank.

Soon a family appeared, dressed in casual Earth clothes. It had to be our Russian counterparts! The blonde, straight-haired man that I assumed to be Vladimir made the first move. He reached out to me with great warmth. Soon all of us Earth adults were embracing, while the children greeted each other more cautiously. I noted that Vladimir's wife, Galima, was South Asian. The Ivanov's also were an inter-racial family, perhaps another part of the Liosan plan.

The crew smiled. As we became aware of our hosts amusedly ogling us, we felt a bit embarrassed. We all looked at each other, not knowing what to say. Then a Liosan woman, of appearance similar to our Iroquois nations, walked majestically toward us. The five gold quarter moons on each of her shoulders probably indicated her high rank. I assumed her to be the commander. She scanned our group, making eye contact with each of us, children included.

"Welcome, Earth friends! How steadfast you have been. We of Planet Lios have depended on your sacrificial assistance to ensure the efficacy of our mission, thereby making it your mission as well."

Her focus was now on me. I stood there wondering if her extra-terrestrial sensitivity allowed her to hear my heart beating. A nudge from Gracie prompted me to find my courage and my voice, and respond,

"To be here as your friends is a great privilege. And, although it didn't seem so in the beginning, the understanding that your mission is also ours came to us with time and experience. We know that it is imperative to help you."

"And you all have – each one of you – Mark, Gracie and Sarah – and Vladimir, Galima, Alexandra and Nikolai. Also, we do not forget your important legal support – Attorneys Chen and Leonov."

"Now forgive me. We know you so well, but you do not know us. I am Commander Janu Lios, chief of the armada squadron over North America, and this is some of our crew."

Noting Sarah's puzzled look, she added, "Sarah, you have a question."

"Well, yeah. You said your last name is Lios. That's the name of your planet, so I wonder about that."

"You were not the only one in your party wondering, but your thought waves came through the strongest. Lios is the family name of all Liosans, because Lios is our mother planet. And, of course, some of us have the same first names. Just like Earth has many 'Sarah's', we have many 'Janu's.' We can identify ourselves by individual telepathic codes when necessary."

"But what about husbands and wives and their children? Don't they share a name?"

"Why yes, they do. Even though we are all one family, we do recognize our more intimate relationships. They are identified by combinative code, like 'sunrise' or 'fox foot'."

Sarah indicated her understanding, as did Natasha and Nikolai.

Each heard the interchange in her/his own language, as did we their parents. It was a learning experience for all of us.

Janu then invited us to tour the rest of the ship and to meet the crew. We followed close behind Janu.

The first section we entered was a dimmed circular space, with seven cylinders, three feet high by three and one half feet in diameter, flashing red, yellow and blue lights.

These, we were told, were navigation sensors, which functioned to detect space debris or alien spacecraft. Six of the cylinders encircled the seventh, in a wheel-like design. About ten feet from the top of the sensors was a domical ceiling, displaying a cosmographic picture of our galactic neighborhood. Janu pointed to the location of Earth, showing its relation to Lios and Nede. This was of great interest to all of us, but the children showed their excitement more outwardly. Even shy little Nikolai managed to say "cool," one of his newly acquired English words.

We then entered a half-circle section. Extending from the half-circle wall were what appeared to be compartments, which I estimated aloud as about two feet high, three feet wide and seven feet in length.

"You have a good eye for measurement," the commander responded. "Here you see sleeping quarters for our male crew. On the other side of the straight wall are sleeping quarters for our female crew. Each section accommodates twenty-seven. The enclosed room to the right of the entrance is accommodation for washing and latrine. The female section is a mirror image of this. The latrines are designed for use in a gravitational area, such as we are now in. Our long weightless journeys through space are accomplished only through dematerialization."

On a limited level, we, of course, were very familiar with the dematerialization/ materialization process. So it was no surprise to hear that our visitors had traveled in this manner. Indeed, how else could they have covered the light-years distance from their planet to ours?

But how was this accomplished? The entire process was a mystery for all of us. It was a mystery when Vladimir and I first experienced much smaller trips through the power of the "force", and it was now an even more powerful mystery.

"You wonder how we travel this way. I am sure that you never took the similar phenomenon in your American television series, *Star Trek*, seriously. In this show and movie, the process was accomplished by a "transporter," a fictional device for dematerialization/materialization, which comes nowhere close to possibility.

"Only when we learned to bring science and spirituality together, did we begin to understand how this might be done. It was, in the measure of your Christian calendar, during the first month of the fifteenth century, that certain seekers of the divine on our planet began to realistically work on this process. These seekers had come to know a practice similar to what some enlightened people on your planet call Kriya Yoga, which opens the door to transcendental power. Within a few years, through transmutation of cells into energy and back again, they developed the gift of dematerialization/ materialization

"Now I know that you have questions about Kriya Yoga. You may have heard of it, since it has been developed on your planet, but I know that you do not understand it. Our methods go beyond it anyway. Perhaps some day there will be time to teach you."

We were now entering their dining section, where an exotic aroma lured our appetites. Seated around a huge elliptical table was the crew, a few of whom we had seen when we first boarded the ship. Together, they must have numbered at least fifty. They snapped to attention as we entered; then responded to Janu's instruction to be at ease. Their facial expressions countered their action suggesting an underlying dark humor – a put-on to mock Earth's militaristic absurdities.

No introduction of us was necessary. As the reconnaissance arm of the "force," they knew us well. They had only to introduce themselves to us, which they did in an unexpected way. Each crew member nodded his or her head in our direction, and telepathically communicated his or her name and specific responsibility. For example, "Temos Lios, navigator." This would not be forgotten, because whenever you looked at him, whether to engage in conversation of just in passing by, his name and role would be instantly remembered.

With the introductions completed, the commander asked us to be seated, for dining and discussion. As guests, my family and Vladimir's family were seated on either side of the commander. The table was elegantly set with fine dinnerware, but the food was nowhere in sight. Janu asked us to bow our heads, as she said grace,

> Omniscient, Omnipotent Creator!
> We give thanks for your bounteous gifts.
> Your love is our source of courage and empowerment.
> Your light guides us in our search for truth, justice, and peace.
> We thank you for our good friends, who serve us and serve you
>   in our mission to Earth.
> Bless this food, that we shall partake of in joyful celebration,
>   as we savor it in praise of you, our God.
> Amen.

The crew accompanied her with an "Ohm" intonation, which we knew we must join. Then, after we all had said another "Amen," we opened our eyes. There before us was a sumptuous spread of food! A vegetarian spread, both familiar and unfamiliar foods, which had materialized while we said grace. Janu explained,

"On your planet, vegetarianism is a matter of individual and group preference, rather than a global exigency. At one time, this was a matter of choice for us as well, but there came a time when officers of our Citizens Service, responsible for protecting positive life, determined that all must follow the vegetarian way, for nutritional, ecological, and spiritual health.

"Beyond what we know of the benefits of a vegetarian diet in personal consumption, we had become aware of the ecology of food production. At one time, our food production had been fueled by a system of profit rather than need. Our resources were being over-exploited in order to produce meat for a privileged minority. Crops cultivated for animal feed threatened the loss of our topsoil, and irrigation sources were running dry because of the great water needs of livestock. Animal waste polluted our streams.

"Before we restructured our economic system, it was taken for granted that there would be 'haves' and 'have-nots.' There were some people of privilege who believed that all had a right to food, but their efforts to feed the hungry were increasingly inadequate. The system itself had to be changed. God provides resources for all his children, not a select few. Once we understood this, we had to learn to use these resources wisely.

"There are, as you know, other reason to be vegetarian. Respect for animals for one, especially when meat production has become dominated by factory farming. But I will stop for now, so that you may better enjoy the food before you, and some informal conversation."

The cuisine was delicious beyond ordinary imagination. While we had listened with great interest to Janu's explanation of their food choice, it was good now to concentrate on our enjoyment of it. The children, in particular, appreciated a break from the monologue. But after we had eaten our fill and the table was cleared, Janu continued,

"I have spoken to you about vegetarianism. We do, however, keep some animals for food production, because, as you have learned from our meal, we use some limited egg and dairy products. Our cows are always grass, not grain fed, and both they and our chickens are free range.

"I must also emphasize that our produce, as you might guess, is free of pesticides, herbicides, and chemical fertilizers, and never genetically modified. Like you, motivated by agribusiness profits, we had developed chemicals for what seemed to be more efficient production. But their negative effects on the health of our population soon became clear, as did the pollution of our earth and waters.

"You are probably surprised that I would spend so much time talking about food. It does, of course, relate to our meal, but more importantly I hope that you can see how our history of relating to this problem can be a model for other problem solving, such as wealth distribution and peace. We must respect life and the planet which nurtures life. Respect cannot come without a change in power relationships. Fortunately, there are those on your planet who, recognizing the seriousness of your situation, are committing themselves to the crucial task of educating the people."

"Educating the people" – a call for commitment, something which we could not ignore; a call for change, a paradigm shift. Janu's discourse on vegetarianism was a parable for revolution. She had been guiding us through a dense wood towards the economic, environmental, political, cultural, moral and spiritual connections between what we eat, how we think, and how we rid the world of war. Janu's smile acknowledged her reading of my thoughts. Then her expression became more somber, giving way to a smile again as her gaze fell on the children. She said,

"As you can see, my feelings are greatly mixed. Your visit with us must come to an end for now, but it is our hope that you will visit us again before our mission is accomplished and we return home. Now you must leave because you have so much urgent work to do on your planet.

"Sarah, Natasha and Nicolai, you were a special joy and enlightenment. Before leaving here, we have arranged for you to meet some of our Liosan children via our virtual reality system. Who knows where that might lead?" That may depend on what you and your parents can accomplish on Planet Earth."

Janu asked Elimsa, one of the female crew, to escort us to the astro-vision room, which was equipped for interplanetary communication. There, although it was especially arranged for kids, we, their curious parents, also had the opportunity to meet the Liosan youngsters and their parents. Like the command ship crew, the families had distinctive beauty. A translation compotent of their interactive computer system enabled us to use their language and ours. We adults enjoyed seeing the children relate so well to each other and hearing them talk about wanting to visits each other's planet. We knew, however, that Earth, still in its state of belligerence, would be a risky place for the children of Lios to visit. Our children, having been part of their parents' struggle, were confident that things would change. They promised to do whatever they could to make a visit from Liosan children possible.

After this interchange, it was time for us to return to terra firma – to do our part in educating and organizing our people and help to create a strategic plan to save our Earth. The temporary tone of our reluctant good-byes made parting easier.

Chapter 32

※———◦———•———※

EMERGING STRUGGLE

Back home in New York and Moscow, our families and friends prepared to take on the daunting task of helping to build consciousness for the essential paradigm shift. We would be in frequent contact with each other for suggestions, evaluation and progress reports. Our operation would be closely monitored by the "force," whose armada had withdrawn to a location protected from Earth's view by a special shield. Not even our most technologically sophisticated space observers could identify their presence. Earthlings who had experienced loss of control now assumed that their power was restored. In reality, this power would continue to be limited by the Liosans until Earth could find a way to move toward a just and permanent peace. If we failed, our visitors would have no choice but to invade, colonize and control our world until we learned. The choice was in Earth's hands.

To begin, there needed to be a change in power relations. For those who now seemingly had no power, power could emerge. "The people united can never be defeated" -- the words of Che Guevara, chanted in protest in many languages since they were first spoken. With few exceptions, however, the people were not united. There could be no power of the many when dependency, false aspiration and ethnic division diverted the masses from the real challenge to their liberation.

There had to be change. Though technology could make it possible to provide for all, false consciousness prevented the sharing of wealth. Vast numbers still lived in dire poverty, while the rich fattened themselves. "Workers of the world" were divided, and too often violence destroyed what little they had.

With most Earthlings believing that our visitors were gone, many did not see the necessity for change. Senator Brinkbane was now emboldened to proclaim that the Liosans had made "a wise decision not to mess with us." He called for an immediate resumption of military deployment. Congresswoman Rivers and her allies, however, believed that the Liosans were still prepared to respond quickly to any such dangerous move.

President Clinton just listened. He clearly understood the choice that had to be made, but was not sure of his support. America's imperialist wars had been possible only through the manipulation of mass consciousness. Could this false consciousness now be healed? What could he say now to turn things around, and how should he say it?

Clinton feared the Brinkbane forces. Brinkbane had many allies. They sat on both sides of the legislative aisles and were a majority among the Joint Chiefs of Staff and on the Supreme Court. They served the interests of corporate leaders and finance capital. It would not be easy. The nation was already into an election year. There had been vigorous assaults on Clinton and on his vice-president, who was campaigning to succeed him. The voting public, except for the progressive counterculture, were in patriotic delusion. Many were vulnerable prey for chauvinistic machination.

Power in Russia had its own chauvinistic machination. Organized crime was now a major influence in its state structure. Globally, workers were divided on their understandings.

Clinton, of course, knew nothing of the role that Vladimir and I would be playing. While many had been out in the streets protesting my incarceration, Clinton had given lip service to the necessity of my arrest, "in the interest of a secure America." That had been his role. Now he knew he had to play a different role. Now he had to consider what our connections to the visitors might mean. Meanwhile, Vladimir Putin, newly in power and challenged by other elements of the Russian power structure, had critical choices to make, as did the rest of the world.

My friend Vladimir and I were faced with an overwhelming responsibility. We had been chosen because we were among those artists who strove to awaken political consciousness. Yet, until our recent notoriety, we had not gotten the audience we had hoped for. But now there was new interest in our work.

Other artists – visual, literary and performing – were also trying to wake people up. Film, a modality that I hoped to learn more about, was especially effective. Usually, art was produced primarily to serve the market.

Could artists instead pull together more healing creativity ?

We set out to brainstorm the question. Telepathically; Vladimir, Galima, Gracie and I began to work on a plan. We would send out a call inviting artists to respond to our urgent situation. But we knew that artists could be full of contradictions. We needed creative minds. Art was a key, but we did not need regressive or irrelevant expression.

"You like to talk about the spiritual, Mark, "Vladimir observed. "Does it belong here?"

Interesting that it was Vladimir who introduced the spiritual. I saw both my art and Vladimir's as spiritual, but had not thought that Vladimir would use that language. Then I remembered that Marx's concern with alienation was spiritual.

"Yes, of course. The spiritual and the material go together. Many in the ruling class want culture to secure their privilege. But there are also wiser heads, who can see that supporting us is also their own salvation. We should get funding."

Our notoriety had made us candidates for leadership. By announcing our continuing role in its mission, the "force" had put us in even greater focus. While many attempted to denigrate our role, others were ready to insure our personal economic independence.

With this support, we adults were able to quit our jobs and devote our energies to organizing. As recognition of our efforts increased, so also did threats against us. Anticipating this, the "force" had insured our safety. Nothing could stand in the way of our mission. Each plot to harm us was foiled in its inception.

Response from the creative community exceeded our hopes. In my own primary discipline, there was already a wealth of work of which most of the world was unaware. Strong visual images against oppression and war and the affirmation of struggle came from many parts of the world, but little Cuba made an especially rich contribution. Liberating work was now shown internationally in the most public places. Music, drama and dance celebrated hope and poetry inspired critical thinking. Film continued to have the most powerful impact. There was a focused effort to show cinema and video that could raise consciousness.

Small viewing and discussion groups gave people an opportunity to share their insights.

Like Vladimir, Galima had taken seriously the words of the "force" on spirituality. "Religion has been a major purveyor of deception." she began. "Vladimir and I see that your faith helps to fulfill you, but most religion has served corrupt power. Authentic spirituality, as your scriptures say, 'makes all things new.'"

To make "all things new" was the challenge. Time was running out and imperialism still held sway. Could we earthlings have turned things around without the intervention of the "force?"

While offers for funding continued to come in, we needed to cull out those that seemed to have problematic agendas. Acceptance of money was never a simple issue. We needed legal advice. Leslie made it clear that this was not her area of expertise. She referred us to another lawyer, Miguel Delgado, whose specialty was advising nonprofit groups. In Russia, Vladimir also found an advisor to screen contributors.

While we adults focused on how best to organize for change; Sarah, Alexandra, and Nikolai were bringing new perspective to their school responsibilities. They still needed to be children, but were having to deal with the hopeful, but nevertheless jarring, awareness of how different their future would be.

For all of us, there was the issue of celebrity. The children became objects of relentless questions from classmates, neighborhood friends and teachers. Within our freshly hired business staff were persons sorting through requests from world leaders and media. Newspapers, magazines, radio and television reporters and talk-show hosts requested interviews. Book publishers and film-makers offered advance payment for exclusive rights to the manuscript of the book they assumed I would write. Merchants and organizers of various causes sought our endorsements.

A demand for my appearance came from the U.S. Congress and for Vladimir's from the Russian Parliament. A representative of the United Nations invited us both to speak. Vladimir and I saw the national engagements as useful. The UN invitation was an opportunity for international contact. Both bodies would open up opportunities for media coverage of our call, so we would not spend too much energy complaining about their limitations.

Miguel had begun receiving major funds on our behalf from some of the more enlightened members of the affluent class, plus smaller donations from ordinary people. He had hired staff, including an important volunteer with considerable experience raising funds for progressive causes. The volunteer was Susan Byrd. She was a wealthy divorcee and patron of the arts, who knew how to connect with venues for performance and for exhibition space. She had a solid social justice history, including that of the recent "Free Mark DeLouise" movement.

Susan believed that people were best awakened in the process of struggle – their own personal struggle and/or in struggles of solidarity. Dependency often led people towards complicity in their own oppression, and fear led them to blame the victim rather than the oppressor. Sometimes art could open new awareness even when facts failed. That made art a key. But even when unlocked, the door could not be opened without struggle.

Vladimir and I sent our joint acceptance reply to the UN. No matter what the Secretary General and the General Assembly might choose, the most powerful governments were controlled by forces of capitalist advantage. We prepared ourselves with this in mind.

Calls came from the few people who knew our unlisted number. Leslie called inviting us to dinner with her and Steve, and then a real surprise – a voice we had not heard in a long time – Jenny Burns. Although I had picked up, Gracie got the cordless right away. After sharing what was happening with our children, Jenny seemed to be moving toward a possible meeting. I hastened to cut this off,

"How's Dan? What's he up to these days?"

Jenny began to run down his feelings of guilt and his wish for reconciliation. We waited to hear more concrete evidence of his repentance, but it was not forthcoming. Jenny said she would talk to Dan, but we knew that would be difficult. Hearing the sadness in Jenny's voice, Gracie responded,

"We can hope. We miss you and will keep you in our prayers."

Just after I hung up, the phone rang again. It was our pastor, Jim Daniels. In church, it had been difficult to communicate with anyone after the service, but Jim said that he was trying to work out a plan for us to share with the congregation. This was another issue for prayer.

Meanwhile, we were considering other venues for communication. Gracie suggested Riverside Church, which had already hosted such luminaries as Martin Luther King and Fidel Castro. We would run this past our promoter, Susan Byrd.

Before we could contact Susan, I received a telepathic communication from Vladimir. He and Galima had connected with a team of experts ready to help them set up a website and apply computer technology to translate our communications into different languages. Together, we would draft our message, calling for redemptive work from creative communities. We would need arts managers to assure that the work reached the masses.

We labored through several drafts of the call until we were both satisfied with the content, degree of exigency and length; then the draft went to our staff for further input. Soon after the approved call went out, responses came in.

As support came in, so did resistance. Desperate to hold on to power, the forces of finance capital became more aggressive. Mainstream media supported their interests, including military buildup and cut backs in civil liberties. But support for us was increasing exponentially. We proceeded steadfastly. Our major target was the many who longed for a better world, but too often were dependent and confused. We had to inspire struggle.

A major task for us and our respective staffs was analysis of the conflicting dynamics. What was the impact of establishment propaganda and how could we counter it? We had to measure our effectiveness and strategize for change.

We were considered treasonous. We were accused of complicity in a plan for extra-terrestrial colonization of our planet. There were some in the privileged class, however, who knew that such a stand could only lead to their own self destruction. Nevertheless, our work continued to be difficult and dangerous.

While our team was operating within the "belly of the beast," Vladimir's team was also at risk. The interests of finance capital were global. Although Russia in some respects had become a "client state," Russian capitalists aspired to similar "success."

Our "teams" continued to monitor the impact of information and misinformation. We noted the responses of various groups to capitalist propaganda and we noted who sought out counter cultural analysis.

Alternative media was now reaching more people than ever.

We had gotten through Y2K. Although many of the world's computers had not been programmed for the new millennium, we had managed to avert chaos in our systems. Yet for some, metaphysical fear remained. It was greed, however, not the supernatural, that was to be feared. The rulers of the world now took comfort in their belief that the extraterrestrials were gone. They claimed that the extraterrestrials who were trying to save us were the enemy.

Soon after the visitors withdrew to their observation point, Earth's rulers found new arguments for their course of exploitation and destruction. Arrogance blinded them to the reality of their own danger, while dependency blinded the masses. If Earth's peoples did not wake up, the Liotians would have to intervene forcibly.

Our hope was that more of humanity would connect with the divine spirit, understand that the "force" was part of this, and unite for change. Even as some who called themselves artists allowed their gifts to be bought out, others were determinedly working for truth. The culture war was intensified. It was expected that when the people began to struggle for justice (however nonviolently), they would be met with violence. Those in the struggle had to be able to defend themselves. The greater the level of mass awareness, strategic organizing and peaceful protest, the less the need for violence. We prayed that the change would be nonviolent, but much depended on our ability to creatively raise awareness. Art was indeed a key.

The impact of our mission was emotionally draining and hard on our families. Vladimir and Galima, as well as Gracie and I, were concerned about the effect this was having on our children. There were some tasks in which it was possible to include them as helpers, and in that process, also as learners. Sarah complained, however, that we did not include her often enough, and that sometimes we seemed so preoccupied that she was afraid to ask questions. Gracie was the first to address the problem,

"Sweetheart, your dad and I are sorry if you feel closed off. This stuff is really weighing us down. How can we do better?"

"You seem to forget that I've been through this since the beginning and I know what it's about. Keeping stuff from me only makes me angry and scared. And, Dad, it really puts me off when you call me 'big girl,' because that's the way you talk to little kids."

I acknowledged that Sarah was right. As a therapist, I should have known better. We also needed to strengthen our faith connections.

"Maybe we all need to pray," I continued. "Let's give thanks for each other, for the "force" and for the strength that God has given us to carry on this struggle."

Chapter 33

* ———————— ✦ ———————— *

THE STRUGGLE CONTINUES

The remaining days, weeks and months of the year 2000 found many of our planet's people shifting their views of the world and of each other. Clinton's vice president, Al Gore, now running for president, had some understanding of the danger we were in, but knew his power was limited. If he were to get the financial support he needed to make the run for president, he could not say what needed to be said. Hoping to get the votes of the majority still tied to the old paradigm, he ran an uninspired campaign. More progressive candidates were largely ignored. The choices were limited.

The election later that year was full of irregularities, particularly in the state governed by the brother of Gore's major contender. This resulted in a contested election, the results of which were decided by a biased Supreme Court, a majority of whose members favored Gore's opponent, George W. Bush. The most regressive elements of the ruling class were thus assured of an administration loyal to their interests.

In the most contested state, thousands were either denied the right to vote or had their ballots discarded. The half-measures of the Democratic challenge to this fraud suggested the complicity of both parties in the coup. Major corporate forces, particularly the oil interests, thus secured political representation for their exploitation of resources and labor, at home and abroad. Whatever military action would be needed to counter resistance would be provided. It was a scenario for unending war, but war needed popular support.

More wars would bring doom, not only to our beautiful planet Earth, but, as our visitors feared, to our galactic neighbors as well. The Pentagon's doctrine of full spectrum dominance laid the foundation not only for global wars, but for the militarization of space.

In order to insure support for massive militarization, effective propaganda was needed. The attacks of 9/11 set this stage. As anger in oppressed regions of the world grew, many groups were inclined to express it in regressive forms, rather than legitimate actions of self defense. Herein lay an opportunity for arousing war sentiment in America, with an act of overwhelming terror. The inspiration for a specific act would be easy to plant, and the enabling of the act could be arranged. The time would be 9/11.

There were many unanswered questions relating to how a regressive group, specifically the Islamic terrorists associated with the 9/11 attacks, could pull off the destruction at the World Trade Center and the Pentagon, unaided by more sophisticated and powerful forces. How could this have happened? How could it have been possible for planes to crash into these normally well protected buildings? Why did the Towers collapse in the manner of controlled demolition? And why, in the summer of 2001, was Osama bin Laden (already America's "most wanted" international criminal) treated by an American surgeon and visited by a CIA agent in Dubai without arrest?

Few could believe that forces within the American government would bring such destruction on its own people. Yet why else would the masses get behind the will to war? War was needed to control Afghanistan, so that a trans-Afghan oil pipeline might be built and global capital could profit from the Afghan drug trade. War was needed to control Iraq oil and reap profits from our military industries. These were motives that most Americans did not want to consider. Instead, they were ready to support aggression against any Islamic nation that our government claimed harbored terrorists.

To further insure mass war support, our government and its press claimed that Saddam Hussein had weapons of mass destruction. When inspectors, however, found no weapons of mass destruction, and it was reported that Saddam and Osama bin Laden were in fact enemies, the public was slow to admit error.

The politics of fear undermined the hope for peace. I remembered the words from John's first epistle, "Perfect love casts out fear, for fear has to do with punishment, and whoever fears has not reached perfection in love." How could this be understood by those who merged God with the state?

It would take an army of creative love to counter fear. Art "warriors" were awakening to their responsibility. In response, people all over the world were becoming aware of how nationalism and tribalism had blinded them. Working with the artists were various socialist groups who were now finding new unity between themselves and the people.

Economic justice for all was increasingly a priority, and the understanding of "human nature" was being liberated from its culture-corrupted definitions. New insights brought hope and "cast out fear." Speakers, seminars, films, books, banners, posters and leaflets were our weapons. Chants, poetry, painting, music, dance and drama also helped raise consciousness.

In order to serve the power interests of a few, the world had put itself on the brink of total disaster. While condemning weaker nations for defensively developing both acknowledged and suspected weapons of mass destruction, the greatest military power in history harbored significant quantities of chemical and biological weapons, and a nuclear arsenal exponentially more capable than its contenders. A majority allowed this to happen. The evil spirit manifested itself in complex ways, but good was finding powerful expression. The battle lines were drawn.

Strategic planning between the DeLouise and Ivanov families

continued through telepathic communication. We were aided by dedicated peace veterans, but were able to go beyond their analysis.

Through invisible espionage, made possible through dematerialization, we could identify danger and determine timely resistance. Those who understood the consequences of inaction focused whatever skills they had to stop Earth's race to destruction. Some also sought strength in prayer.

On Sunday, we went to church. It was February 9, 2003. All eyes seemed to follow us as we walked to our seats. The collective anxiety of the congregation was palpable. Many, struggling for normalcy, nodded their greetings in our direction. Jim Daniels headed toward us, Bible in hand. Following his friendly greeting to us all, he turned to me with a request,

"Mark, would you be willing to do our scripture reading today?"

I had already noted his topic as "Out of Babylon." The reading was selected verses from Chapter 18 of Revelation.

"Sounds right," I said. "I'll do my best."

I was not surprised by Jim's choice. It was a chapter I had never known to be in the lectionary, but this was the second time I had known Jim to choose it. His first time had been shortly after the opening of "Ten of Each." I believed that Jim was one of the few preachers who seemed to understand the reading, which is so misused that it is generally avoided in the liberal church. I knew, however, that Jim understood the symbolism and, as he had proven when he used the text shortly after I first exhibited my "Number 10" at Westbeth. I looked forward to new connections that he might make between New Testament times and today.

> ... Fallen, fallen is Babylon the great! ...
> Come out of her my people,
> so that you do not take part in her sins,
> and so that you do not share in her plagues;
> for her sins are heaped high as heaven,
> and God has remembered her iniquities

What we were witnessing today, again brought to mind Revelation's fallen Babylon, and God calling His people out of her. But now, it seemed, we might be closer to a real paradigm shift. Those who today were protesting against war and connected iniquities of this Babylon were, in spirit, coming out of her evil control. At the same time, we were strengthening ourselves to bear the pain and suffering this Babylon's fall would bring; while anticipating celebration for redemptive victory won.

The world was in pain. Expenditures for the military-industrial complex had increased exponentially, while human needs were ignored. Devastating poverty afflicted large areas of the globe, while the criminal economy thrived. Violence, both economic and military, prevailed.

As our creative movement grew, so did the attacks on our credibility. To counter our efforts, the imperialists found other "artists" who served their needs, using their skills to paint the oppressors as defenders of democracy and guardians against terror. In defense, we needed the resources of experienced movement analysts and organizers.

There were, of course, some who considered themselves artists who worked neither for or against us, but simply could not focus on the structural crisis. It was as if they thought that re-arranging the furniture could put out the fire in a burning house. Yet, increasingly, the energy was on our side.

Many had hoped that the next election would bring change. The Democrats had chosen John Kerry to challenge President Bush, but those who understood the urgency of our situation knew that he was not the answer. Nevertheless, Bush had to be stopped, and Kerry was the lesser of evils. To our dismay, however, Bush won again in another fraudulent election, corrupted by blatant irregularities in the voting process.

On January 20, 2005, Bush addressed the nation, marking the beginning of his second term. He understood his victory as a mandate to escalate imperial mission and to further policies that polarized rich and poor in the name of "freedom." National policies would serve the interests of corporate greed and threaten ultimate destruction.

As long as power was still in the hands of a system based on exploitation, Earth itself, as well as its inhabitants, was under attack. The increasing destructiveness of hurricanes, tornadoes, and tsunamis was a warning that continued violence to Earth and to each other would lead to our demise. Global warming could not be a priority for those focused on surviving the battles of capitalist competition.

War, in fact "endless war," could be the only result. And war included the possibility of nuclear annihilation.

One evening, exhausted by our demanding responsibilities of brainstorming, organizing, educating, demonstrating, etc., Gracie and I returned home from a meeting on 14th Street with fish-and-chips take-out to share with Sarah. After a late supper we were all ready for bed.

As tired as I was, adrenalin was still running through my system, and I could not sleep. Frustration and anger made me sit up in bed with a fury that awakened Gracie. I complained about the Friday night party noise, but we both knew that this was not my only problem. We had expressed confidence that everything would work out right, in keeping with the tripartite co-operation between DeLouise, Ivanov and the "force." But beneath this there was a nagging "what-if?," asking about all the things that might go wrong.

We knew that the deepest of faith is constantly subject to challenge. Wanting to help ease our strained emotions, Gracie tenderly suggested that we get up and talk things out, over some relaxing chamomile tea.

As we climbed down out of our sleeping loft, I felt an irresistible urge to look out our windows.

Gracie came to stand beside me. What we saw, shining brilliantly in the northwestern sky, was the phenomenal star that had so amazingly changed our lives when my story began. We looked at each other in astonishment. Gracie trembled with excitement and said,

"I've got to go and wake Sarah. We can't let her miss this!"

Gracie ran to get Sarah, while I stayed at the window transfixed, praying that the star wouldn't move before they came. I heard them bounding down the stairs, but it didn't seem fast enough, so I called on them to hurry. Sarah was first to reach the window. Excitedly she grabbed my arm and shouted,

"Wow! It has to be them!"

Before any of us could say another word, the star suddenly moved, not in our direction as it had before, but up and out, further into space. Then the stars in the sky as far as we could see seemed to proliferate in number, growing brighter and brighter, moving closer and closer, until stopping at about the same distance as the one we first saw.

I was sure that Vladimir and his family had or would experience a similar sighting. Because they were on the other side of Earth and several hours ahead of us, our sightings could not be simultaneous. If Vladimir and his family had already seen the "star," he might not have wanted to contact us until we could share the experience. As I wondered whether or not I should call Vladimir now, I heard the familiar voice of the little Orb. I could not see him, but he spoke the brief message, "Speak to Vladimir." Immediately I told Gracie and Sara that we should all telepathically connect with Vladimir and his family. They had indeed seen the star. Joyously, we exchanged our experiences. Then we agreed that there was not much more to do than to watch for its next moves and await its instructions.

While adult heads were thinking in these terms, our little Sarah, and perhaps little Alexandra in Russia, were curious about how aware the rest of the world had become about what was happening in the skies above us. Sarah went to the computer to search the Internet, while we scanned the TV and radio, searching for breaking news. But there was nothing there. That seemed strange until we realized from our experience what the "force" was doing. It was using its power to blight Planet Earth's space observation technology, and permitting only its allies to see that it had arrived. Our planet's most powerful negative elements – the corporate rulers and their servants in government and industry -- would be taken by surprise at the very moment they believed their hegemony was complete, their hoped-for consequence of racist, profit-seeking wars.

While so many in our world shuddered in fear of the extra-terrestrial presence, we were reassured by our familiar little messenger and friend. The "force" had again sent the little Orb to assure us that all would be well. We still did not know how this would be. Would our work be realized through the power of the people? Or would it be necessary for the "force" to intervene once more? We had successfully fulfilled our covenantal commitment to inspire many of Earth's peoples. But we could not rest until we saw critical mass working to assure peace for ourselves and for our galactic neighbors. The struggle continued.